ISLA MALDITA

Isla Maldita

A Fable of Puerto Rico in 2045

Sebastian Faust

Atabey Press
New Port Richey, Florida
Copyright © 2023 by Atabey Press

First Edition

ISBN: 979-8-9877112-3-1 (ebook)
ISBN: 979-8-9877112-4-8 (paperback)

For those who remain, because they deserve better

DISCLAIMER

This is a work of speculative fiction. Names, characters, places, and incidents are either the product of the author's imagination, or are used fictitiously. Any resemblance to actual persons, living or dead; events, or locales is entirely coincidental. The timelines are a blend of documented history and speculative predictions intended solely for entertainment purposes. This novel is not intended to serve as a source of historical information, or future predictions. It is only intended to entertain, and generate constructive dialogue.

A Recent Political History of Puerto Rico

2008: Former Governor Aníbal Acevedo Vilá is indicted on 19 counts of campaign finance violations, wire fraud, and conspiracy. Subsequently acquitted of all charges, the scandal casts a shadow on his political career.

2009 Former Senator Jorge de Castro Font is sentenced to five years in Federal prison after being convicted of 20 counts of bribery, wire fraud, and money laundering related to accepting bribes for political favors.

2010: FBI's Operation Guard Shack, a multi-year investigation into the corruption in the Puerto Rico Police Department, leads to over 130 arrests of members of the PR Police and Justice Departments

2016: Governor Alejandro Garcia Padilla declares the island unable to pay its debt, which exceeds $70 billion. The U.S. Congress responds by passing the PROMESA Act, which places the island's finances under the control of a Federally appointed Financial Oversight and Management Board (FOMB).

July 2019: Former Education Secretary Julia Keleher is

arrested alongside five other people on charges of steering federal money to unqualified, politically connected contractors.

August 2019: Governor Ricardo Rosselló resigns after two weeks of massive protests triggered by the leak of hundreds of pages of racist, abusive, and profane chats between Rosselló and his aides. Leaked chat transcripts suggest the Governor directed consultants —paid with taxpayer funds—to persecute political enemies, and uncovered evidence of widespread corruption and mishandling of the response to Hurricane Maria.

December 2019: Governor Wanda Vázquez Garced faces various scandals during her short tenure, including allegations of improper influence in hiring and procurement processes, and handling of government contracts. The *Puerto Rico Incentives Code*, or Act 60, consolidates the island's tax haven laws into one statute, pointedly scaling back government oversight of residency, documentation, and investment requirements.

2020: Governor Pedro Pierluisi is elected Governor. Several key members of his administration, to include the Secretary of State, are holdovers from the Rosselló administration. Former Governor Wanda Vázquez is arrested on Federal bribery charges related to her failed 2020 campaign.

2022: Six Municipal mayors are arrested across the island in an FBI sting operation. FBI agents also arrest Rep. María Milagros "Tata" Charbonier, the former head of Puerto Rico's House Ethics Committee, who was charged in a public corruption case involving her son, husband and assistant.

2023: The government of Puerto Rico claims to pass the first of five balanced budgets, required by Federal Law to remove FOMB oversight of the island's finances. In the absence of any audited financial statements, the US Government questions the validity of the claim.

PART ONE
TOMORROW

PUERTO RICO, 2045. TWENTY SEVEN YEARS AFTER HURRICANE MARIA

2027: Puerto Rico's population drops by 250,000 from the benchmark during Hurricane Maria. The influx of wealthy transplants begins to visibly alter the island's economy and housing market, with local residents being priced out. The percentage of the population relying on government assistance climbs 6% due to lack of job opportunities and economic stagnation.

2031: Energy costs are 51% higher than the average in the continental US, impacting both residential and commercial sectors. The Legislature passes a law providing energy rebates to Act 60 residents in order to "incentivize economic growth." The student-teacher ratio stands at 42 to 1 in public schools, although actual data is difficult to obtain. Waste management becomes a critical issue as every landfill on island is operating beyond capacity, leading to the San Juan metro area suffering from the worst Air Quality Index outside of Beijing or Caracas, Venezuela.

2035: The mismanagement of disaster recovery funds becomes front-page news in the mainland US, after the GAO publishes a report that 87 cents out of every recovery dollar has been allocated to firms all related to a single, well-connected lobbyist. When the lobbyist is arrested by the FBI in a pre-dawn raid, Congressional representatives from New York, New Jersey, Florida and Ohio push emergency legislation stripping the FBI of funding for further investigations. Puerto Rico becomes a global economic curiosity by having the highest number of billionaire residents per capita, while the mean per-capita income drops below 10% of the US average.

2039: The disparity between the wealthy transplants and local residents becomes stark, with 30% of residential properties, and 60% of commercial properties, owned by Act 60 expats. A majority of the population is now dependent on some form of welfare assistance, straining government resources. Labor participation rate drops below 25%.

2042: The labor participation rate plummets below 20%, with a significant portion of the population either unemployed or underemployed. The Legislature unanimously votes an income tax increase, with a specific exemption for Act 60 residents. The primary education system has effectively collapsed, with the majority of schools closed, and student teacher ratios stabilizing only due to a massive exodus to the mainland US. Pollution becomes a health emergency when over-capacity landfills spontaneously ignite due to methane outgassing. A solar energy bill, which would remove all taxes on renewable energy, is defeated in the Legislature, who instead passes a bill approving a fifty-year concession for diesel fuel to a startup company run by a former governor's daughter. The current Governor promptly signs the bill into law.

2045: An education bill seeking to close and demolish empty schools — increasingly used for homeless shelters, human and organ trafficking, and drug distribution — fails in the Legislature, which cites "Cultural Heritage" as the reason. "Riñonero" ("kidney harvester") becomes the third-hottest job for public housing residents, just below human trafficking and meth production. Legions of unemployed youth scouring streets for homeless people, targeting immigrants from Venezuela and Ecuador. Kidneys with the correct genetic match are in hight demand by Act 60 residents suffering from diabetes, fetching up to $5000 on the black market. Fortaleza dismisses these reports as "fabrications of the opposition party." The Legislature fails to pass the first balanced budget since the introduction of the Financial Oversight and Management Board in 2016.

ONE

THE ENGINES THROTTLED BACK, slowing the jet below transonic on the descent into San Juan. Isabel Perez gazed at the brilliant ocean and emerald hills and caught her breath. She imagined a different scene twenty-seven years ago, days after her birth, hours before Hurricane Maria devastated Puerto Rico, when her parents took her from a birthplace she never expected to return.

Until today.

The SST, wings swept forward for the approach, descended over the outskirts of an island simmering in glorious disorder. Gray sprawl emerged from the vibrant green of lush forest, dotted with blue tarps in various shades of age. Closer still, traffic choked the roads. A thousand roofs, mottled with black mold, clustered around infrequent islands of the solar collectors that covered every structure back in Tampa.

She wondered if one might belong to Titi Luisa, the aunt she hadn't seen since her *quinceañera* a decade ago. Luisa, as wide as she was tall, survived Hurricane Maria's wrath huddled in her childhood home. Reliving that history through photos and holos had never been enough. Isabel had not returned to her birthplace since age five.

The landing gear protested as the craft touched down and rumbled down the tarmac, using every inch of runway to decelerate. Long wings swept back, their tips cycling up and down from the buckled pavement as they taxied to the terminal. The jet, a routine sight back home, seemed outsized and unwelcome in the shimmering heat.

She disembarked into the humidity, blossoming into a sweat despite the cool fog emanating from the aircraft's frozen metal skin. The smells hit her first: decay from rot, coffee, and pastries, a wisp of flowers, and something that burned. Then the noise: traffic, rock doves, and something beyond, perhaps surf and the comfort of the sea. Clouds fractured the deep blue sky, taming the stinging assault of the sun.

She stepped into the terminal and entered a forgotten world. Everything and everyone moved in a dull roar. Families smiled with anticipation and relief, adults talked animatedly on handsets, professionals acted busy and important. Everyone seemed to reach out and smile, holding onto the fabric of life with palpable energy. The arrival lounge reminded her of the Puerto Rican *cafetines* sprouting all over Tampa, testaments to a twenty-year exodus from the island that had yet to ebb. The smells—coffee and bread and tobacco and sweat and life—covered her like rain.

She stopped at a deli for a *quesito*, a rolled pastry with sweet cheese and sugar glaze, her favorite delicacy. None of her payments worked when she flashed her chip at the cashier. Her glasses listed the options—cash, something she hadn't seen since her first kiss— and a local crypto she'd never heard of. She chose that one, paid through her backup coin account, stunned to find the treat cost more than lunch back home.

"*Disculpe*," she asked the squat woman behind the counter. "Is this right?"

The lady nodded, sneering in expectation of cancelling the transaction. "*La deuda.*"

The debt. For the rest of their lives, everyone born on the island was doomed to pay for the excesses of decades past. How anyone might afford one of these delicacies escaped her. Her first economic interaction had been disjointed—exactly as she'd been warned.

She thought of the reason for the trip as she walked towards the baggage claim area. A few months ago, she landed the job of her dreams: a nonprofit advocating for the growing diaspora of displaced Puerto Ricans living in the US. When Isabel spoke about political inequality and climate justice, the director cut her off. The woman, visibly tired through the holo, was brutal and succinct: "We only have room for the facts. Go to the island and see for yourself. You'll start when you return."

Isabel protested, replying with selections from months of research. Her future boss nodded politely, then reminded her of the Balkanization of national news. "You of all people should know just how biased the news has become," she nodded with a sad smile. "Your birthplace is no different. Do you really believe that the Puerto Rico you see online is the truth?"

The blunt retort was shocking and rational. Isabel, already a heavy user of social media filtering, redoubled her skepticism. No more curated media, glossy tourist holos, or precious white papers from idealist think tanks. Seconds after finishing the call, she booked flights to visit her Aunt Luisa. Whether on vacation or research, she'd spend a week immersed in the island of her birth. The anticipation of the unfiltered experience now filled her with a vague sense of dread.

She thought of that and more as she passed dozens of video ads promising adventure, luxury, and pampering in slick clips augmented by AI. The images, she noticed, did not include anyone who appeared local. Every AR ad superimposed on her glasses advertised an island at odds with her surroundings. Her soon-to-be

7

boss had been right: something was off, and she had to see it for herself.

She muted the incessant ads with a flick, ignoring the barrage of images of an island cosplaying as paradise. The Duty-Free area loomed steps past the lift to baggage claim. The AR on her glasses lit up once more, this time with offers superimposed on all manner of kitsch, liquor, and jewelry. Bottles of imported rum for a day's wages, perfumes no one back home could afford, goods meant to showcase opulence at the expense of practicality. The prices were high for Tampa, and stratospheric for what she'd experienced over the past ten minutes.

The soft ping of the lift rescued her from the excess. She exited into a chaotic baggage claim area, with two belts delivering suitcases of all sizes. Her glasses showed no timeline or location where hers might arrive. Then a small glowing arrow popped up: US PASSPORT ONLY. A handful of her fellow travelers waited around a belt carrying a few boxes, while the rest stood around an empty carousel with a sign reading PASAPORTE LOCAL.

"Excuse me," Isabel tapped a gruff-looking young woman with body armor and neck tattoos.

"Diga?"

"I think those people were on my flight."

The woman nodded.

"Why are there two different lines?"

She answered in perfect English. "US passport there, locals over here."

"What does that mean? I thought we all had the same passport. US passports?"

The woman laughed, as if told a sad joke. Isabel was about to ask why when her glasses flashed, notifying her of her bag's arrival.

She popped the wheels out and followed the RIDESHARE signs to an area outside. A wet heat slammed into her, a pungent wave of dead vegetation carried on the salt breeze. People surrounded her: a round woman kissing a tired old man; two middle-aged women squealing in delight meeting an old friend; a wrinkled man enveloped by a younger woman masked with tears. The raw emotion of families and friends reunited tore at her heart. She, too, would meet a loved one soon.

Isabel tapped her glasses and swiped through several apps, looking for transportation, when she noticed a paper sign taped on a light post. An outdated square made of dots—QR codes, if she remembered her mom's stories—clung to a metal light post. The glass recognized it after a few seconds. She blinked to accept, justifying the inconvenience as support for the local economy.

Most of her fellow passengers had left by the time a sedan with flickering orange headlights rumbled up. It smelled like it ran on gasoline, something abolished long ago in Tampa. Cars running on fossil fuel? Progress had eliminated engine smoke, remaining only in Texas, Idaho—and apparently San Juan. The only way to bring gasoline to an island was by ship. Expensive pollution, to create more expensive pollution. Was her island still importing fossil fuels to power cars when half the world drove EVs?

She shook her head at the thought and nodded at the driver. He was young, with the hard part, sculpted eyebrows, and chains typical of petty dealers back in Ybor City. She was about to wrestle her bag inside when a hand clamped on her shoulder. A woman, with eyes as sharp as her tone, barked at the man.

"*¡Ella viene conmigo!*" she spat before slamming the door shut and pulling Isabel back.

The young man pulled out something shiny and black. A gun? Isabel froze. The kid flashed the lady the middle finger, yelled something profane, and sped off.

"I'm sorry, do I know you?"

"Cancel your ride," the woman snapped. "Now."

"Señora, I'm sorry but—"

"Cancel it!"

She stood back, shocked at the woman's demand, and cancelled the request with a blink. No penalty for the cancelled pickup.

"Did you cancel?"

"I did. Why did you do that?"

"Don't tell me—You're from Orlando?"

She stiffened at the affront. "Tampa. But I was born here. Cupey."

"Ah. Well, don't get in any of those," she said and pointed at the flyer. "You would have arrived at your house with one less kidney."

"He was going to take my kidney?" She snorted a derisive chuckle. "Oh, please."

"You have been gone a long time. Why do you think all the rich expats come to Puerto Rico? It isn't just to avoid paying taxes, *mija.*"

"I'm sorry, what? You're crazy!"

The woman grimaced, as if saying "what did you expect?" and glanced back at a younger woman a few paces from them, who nodded in assent.

Isabel's insides lurched. "Are you serious?"

"*Sí.*" Both women nodded, disgust palpable in their stares. This wasn't a convoluted tourist trap, or some trick. Their eyes bled with anger and shame.

"Well, should we call the police?" She scanned the area, looking for help, and found none.

The older woman touched a warm palm to Isabel's arm. "*Ay bendito. Tan inocente.*" She squeezed her hand and gestured the sign of the cross. "The police will do nothing. Much has changed since you left, mija. *Que Dios te bendiga.*"

Then they left to meet a nervous man with a thin mustache emerging from a tangle of beat-up cars, and disappeared into a gentle, misting rain.

Two

Isabel stepped back into the dry safety of the terminal and tapped her glasses. She could not believe the women's admonition, but the eyes of the young driver haunted her. The bizarre encounter had delayed her too close to work traffic, and Luisa had warned her to do everything possible to avoid "*el tapón.*" She played it safe and chose a US based rideshare. Several EVs were only minutes away. She selected a ride, noticing an option for something unexpected: security. The information was stark:

Armed, bonded driver/operators for elevated threat areas.

Spooked by the women's warnings, she accepted the surcharge and added something in the comments.

I'm back after a long time, and unfamiliar with the neighborhoods.

She figured that bit of personal information would be innocuous.

After a brief wait, a large black SUV, a cross between a limo and a military vehicle, whined up to the curb. The light rain had stopped, bathing the afternoon in a steamy heat smelling of burnt metal. She stepped close to the vehicle as a handsome man sporting a neatly trimmed beard, killer sunglasses, and dark gray body armor lowered the window.

"Isabel?"

She nodded and stared at the bulletproof vest. The man waved his watch by hers and read her ID before breaking into a smile.

"Cupey, huh?"

She nodded again and allowed him to load her bag in the back seat. The heavy doors closed with less a click than a thump, and she settled into the cool, comfortable interior.

"First time back?"

"Yes." She gazed outside as they left the airport behind and entered Baldorioty Avenue. The boulevard, pockmarked with holes and debris, reminded her of reels of conflicts in Somalia or Azerbaijan. Cars missing wheels, doors, or engines dotted the sides of the road, and white crosses popped up like mushrooms, almost hidden by the ever-present weeds. She counted at least three masses covered in dirty cloth, which she hoped were not bodies.

"The lady back there... she told me about a black market for organs?"

"*Los riñoneros.*" His smile did not involve his eyes. "A lot of the Act 60 people have diabetes."

"The what?"

"You haven't been back lately, have you?"

She shook her head, hoping he'd continue.

"There are three Puerto Ricos," the man said. "Ten percent of the people are rich beyond your imagination." He pointed behind himself at the gleaming luxury hotels of Isla Verde, sparkling in the afternoon sun. "Stateside millionaires move here under this law called Act 60, promising to invest in exchange for paying no taxes. They never do. But the government lets them get away with anything because they need the bribes."

Then he indicated to decrepit high-rises over Santurce. Their outdated architecture, dark concrete, and decay were clear from a distance. "Those shitholes are filled with the twenty percent of Puerto Ricans like me who actually work, usually to make the expats money." Finally, he pointed to his left. Isabel struggled to find what he meant until she understood he was pointing at a faded yellow apartment complex covered in graffiti. Curtains flapped from broken windows, and gnarled guardrails dangled from tiny balconies. An entire corner of one building, perhaps six stories tall, had crumbled to the ground below.

"The rest live in places like those. The government has kept them unemployed for three generations, living *del mantengo*."

He adjusted the rear-view mirror to look her in the eye. "Organ harvesting for the rich is one way out of that hell."

Isabel tried to swallow. "I thought that only happened in the third world."

"Happens all over the Caribbean and Central America. You would've been fine. As soon as he scanned your passport, he would've stolen your luggage and dropped you off somewhere. They look for migrants and locals, not US citizens."

"That's still sick!"

"Well, it is better than being unemployed your entire life." He pointed at another tenement tucked across the avenue from a bombed-out grocery store. "Two-thirds of Puerto Rico live like that."

"Seventy percent of the island doesn't work?"

"Eighty percent don't pay taxes," he corrected. "This is the last tax shelter for the American dream."

She winced at the reminder of the injustice. For decades, Puerto Rico had been a tax haven for those not born here. Many decried the practice when it created what everyone expected: a failing system of haves and have nots. But the digital fog of thousands of competing narratives attenuated the indignation, condemning every outrage into fading memory. She'd been an unwilling accomplice to the submissive act of forgetting. The admonitions of her soon-to-be boss—go see for yourself—now rang with a wisdom she found prescient. The scene outside—gleaming commercial buildings rising from crumbling concrete, the overpowering stench of garbage, the haze of smoke and pollution—was far removed from the airport holos welcoming tourists to her island. Words her mother spoke years ago now made sense, cutting through the discomforting blanket of noise that hid the island's truth from an unsuspecting world.

La isla está enferma, y no creo que se recupere. The island is sick and may never recover.

"How long can this last?" Isabel whispered.

The man chuckled. "Hopefully long enough for you to see your family."

She grabbed her wrist, covering her chip and her watch. "How do you know I'm visiting family?"

He stared through the rear-view mirror. "You didn't know about *los riñoneros.* You're not doing lines of coke in the back seat. And I'm taking you to a neighborhood that time forgot."

She sat back, absorbing the man's response. She'd been a dreamer, yearning for the culture and landscapes and stories she savored while growing up. Witnessing reality firsthand rekindled a hidden fear: that she'd been born at the apex of Puerto Rico's history, that the island's best days were in the past.

The car pulled through a decrepit checkpoint, where a bored woman waved them through a useless gate. The driver flashed a piece of cardboard Isabel imagined to be a physical ID—something she hadn't seen since she was five—and weaved around abandoned cars and through a neighborhood she'd seen a dozen times in VR. Those holos, depicting neat homes and vibrant streets, had been captured long before today. Most homes sported strange corrugated metal awnings. Holes pockmarked the cracked pavement, and ripped bags disgorged garbage onto the sidewalks. The pop of fireworks ebbed and flowed as they weaved to her destination.

They arrived at a familiar-looking, modest house. Paint peeled off the sides and roof, but tidy garden planters blossomed with life. She tried to open the car door, and nothing happened. A shard of ice sliced through her.

"I need to get out. Please."

The man must've sensed her tension. "I'm sorry. Just waiting." He tapped the center display, an overlay of their location surrounded by red circles contracting into points. Something popped on the sidewalk, like a tiny burst of hail.

"What was that?"

"Bullets. Idiots shooting into the air. Should be over soon."

Isabel stared at the screen. Dozens of red dots surrounded them, the closest several blocks away. Those had not been fireworks. A metallic pop on the roof startled her.

"People are shooting guns in plain daylight? Why don't the police do something about that?"

The man bent over in laughter. "You're really not from here, huh?" He flashed a sad smile. "It'll be only a few more minutes."

"How do you know where they're at?"

"Acoustic sensors." He pointed at the hood. "Surplus military equipment from Azerbaijan."

"Why don't the police use that to find them?" She craned her neck to look at driveways pockmarked with tiny craters. "That's dangerous. They might kill someone."

This time, the man turned. "Because the police aren't allowed to use this. Too expensive. And worse, it would," he made air quotes, "violate the *rights* of the shooters."

"But people could be hurt!"

He shook his head. "People die here by the hour. They should pick up those bodies you saw on the highway in a few days, before they start to stink. Most of them are gunshots. Don't worry. Not all of them are from above."

She tried to answer, but nothing came out. She squeezed the

door handle, dug her nails into her hands to feel something, anything. This was not the Puerto Rico she'd imagined.

The dots coalesced, then moved away. "Alright. They're off to another shootout. Let's go."

"How did you get this? Why do you have this stuff?"

"I was an Army Ranger. Came back to drive rich tourists. Good living."

"You do more than drive, don't you?"

He pulled out a handgun and Isabel froze. "The right passport gets you a lot of extra rights down here. And lets you make some good money." He holstered the gun as the doors opened, then dragged Isabel's roller bag from the back seat. She understood, for the first time, the soft popping sounds far away. The metal over-hangs by the entrance of every home made uncomfortable sense.

"Keeps the lead rain off you," the man said with a wink.

Titi Luisa, smaller and wider and more lovely than she could've imagined, opened the door and spread her arms.

"¡Isabel, mi sobrina adorada! ¡Bienvenida a la Isla del Encanto!"

THREE

"TITI LUISA!"

Isabel fell into the Luisa's soft embrace, and felt her aunt's ancient hands caress her face.

"Dios mío, you are more beautiful than any picture. Ven. Estás flaca."

Luisa waved at the driver, locked the door behind her and led them into the kitchen. The inside of the house lay in cool stillness, soft with the scent of candles, sweet bread, and local spice. Iron bars cast lazy shadows through hurricane shutters. Isabel propped her bag against a wall and breathed in the scent of a home-cooked meal.

"Que Dios te bendiga, mi bella. How was your trip?" Luisa stuck a wooden spoon into a pot and stirred. "Are you hungry?"

"I am so hungry. What did you make?"

"Arroz con cebolla. Your favorite."

Isabel sat down to a heavy plate. Her aunt piled the dish—rice sautéed with onion, bacon, and spices until salty and sweet—next to a stack of *tostones*, golden fried plantains still steaming from the pan.

"You still like jugo de tamarindo? It was your favorite when you were a little girl. Your mother told me they have it in Florida."

Isabel's mouth watered. Food had been the love language of the island for all of her life. Her mother might have lost her touch cooking Puerto Rican delicacies after decades on the mainland. Titi Luisa, Gracias a Dios, had not. Isabel gorged herself, burning her palate, washing it down with tamarind juice and garlicky mayo ketchup.

They chatted about family, Isabel's friends, and history, and she felt at home.

"So what do you think of your birthplace?" Titi Luisa asked.

Isabel swallowed hard and took a sip of the sweet, tart juice. "I learned about riñoneros."

"Ay Dios mío, que vergüenza."

"Titi, that is horrible!" She put her fork down. "No one hears about any of this back in Tampa. What are the police doing about it?"

"Ay bendito, mija," Luisa said, stroking her hand. "Nada. They can't."

"What do you mean, they can't? Don't they know?"

"Yes, but... there's a lot of bad people out there, you know?" She lowered her voice and leaned in. "And *los sesenta* don't want things to change."

"That is no excuse, Titi. Migrants are being cut up like meat on our island. Where are the police?"

"They work for less than minimum wage. You know that. They're not going to stop them. Not when someone is merely hurt."

"Some lady told me people are being butchered!"

Luisa nodded. "It's not like they're doing it for fun. The riñoneros are desperate, but they are filling a need. People need kidneys and lungs for transplants. Some say they save lives."

"Whose lives?"

Luisa turned away, mumbling in shame. "*Los sesenta.* The rich people in Dorado. Their money keeps Puerto Rico running."

"What about the victims? What if I was one of them?"

"You wouldn't." She pointed at Isabel's watch. "You have the right passport."

"So do you."

"I don't." She shook her head. "Mine is local."

"Titi, you're an American citizen. Puerto Rico might not be a state, but it is part of the US. And we have rights. You have rights."

"We can't vote for the president."

"You can if you come to the mainland. But that's not the point. You can't live like this..."

"Why would I want to move away? I've lived here all my life." She winked at Isabel. "Besides, no one is going to take my kidneys. They're too old!"

"Titi, don't say that." She squeezed her aunt's hand. "It would be easier to move to Tampa and be close to your sister. You'd have a lot more opportunities in Florida."

"Your mother can't stop talking about that. We have opportunities here. Why don't you come back?"

That was it. The inevitable question every son and daughter of the island had to answer in their lifetime.

"Titi, I'd love to. But what I saw today makes me wonder."

"That's just one day. It'll get better."

"When?" Isabel pointed to the overhanging metal roof. "Titi, you live in a cage with armor over you because of crime and guns. I saw three dead people laying on the side of Baldorioty. The air is thick with smoke and decaying garbage."

She took a deep breath and clenched her jaw. "Mom told me all about this, and I never believed her. None of this makes the reels back home. I've been here a few hours and now I see what she meant. Politicians have promised for years that everything will be fixed, and it never does. No one believes them anymore. Why stay?"

She shook her head and continued before Luisa could answer. "I know why. Because despite all that, you love it here. You love the food and the people and our history and our customs. But people also need safety and health. The government keeps promising them, but never delivers. And you,"—she rubbed Luisa's wrinkled hand—"are not getting younger."

"*Juventud, divino tesoro. Te vas para no volver.*"

Isabel laughed. "We all grow older, Titi. Please come back. With me."

"You came all the way down here to bring me back? La macacoa?"

"No. I came to be with you. I miss you."

She caressed Isabel's cheek with trembling hands. "You were always kind, and strong, and wise. *La más sabia de tu familia.* I knew it the day you were born. And now you are the most beautiful."

Then she leaned over and slapped her on the hip. "But you are too skinny. Let me get you some *tembleque.*"

Isabel squeaked a grin. "Oh my god, you are so sweet! Yours is my favorite!"

"It's in the fridge. Let me go to the bathroom, and you can tell me all about all the boys who must be crazy about you."

She rolled her eyes as Luisa disappeared down the tiled hallway. The tembleque—translucent, sweet coconut pudding, sprinkled with cinnamon—cooled in a heavy glass dish that must've been decades old. She wondered how much longer Luisa might be able to lift it, living alone without help.

She pulled out plates and spoons from the cupboards when the sound of a crash startled her.

"Titi?"

Silence.

She dashed to the hallway, cold with panic. The old wood veneer door to the bathroom lay ajar. Isabel pushed and found her Aunt Luisa—the strongest, kindest woman she'd ever met—lying on the floor, blood seeping from her nose.

FOUR

"TITI! Titi Luisa! Can you hear me?"

Isabel shook her aunt's hands, felt a faint pulse through the cold skin.

She fought the empty weight and the shakes, tapped on her glasses, and stared at the EMERGENCY icon in the corner. A red bar lit up.

> BLINK TWICE OR SWIPE FOR EMERGENCY.

She blinked a dozen times, swiping the red swoosh on her watch for good measure. She needed a teledoc now.

> OUT OF COVERAGE. BLINK THREE TIMES
> FOR SATELLITE CALL.

If she couldn't even get a damn emergency call—

She glanced at the hot corner of the glasses and heard the comforting ping of the assistant.

"Emergency. I need emergency medical. Doctor or AI."

Acid panic shot through her. She'd never heard of a place without immediate access to medical care.

"Dial 911."

She said a silent prayer when the phone connected, old style, through the cell network instead of through the mesh.

"Emergencia. ¿Necesita asistencia?"

"Sí!" she yelled into the surrounding air. "Please. My titi just passed out."

"Does she have a pulse?"

Isabel held Luisa's hands again. "Yes. It's faint." Somewhere in her mind, she wondered why anyone hadn't asked her for her aunt's vitals through her watch.

"Any bleeding, or—"

"She's bleeding a little through her nose."

"Okay, she may be having a stroke."

Calm, followed by fear. The horror had a name.

"Can you send an ambulance? I sent you my location."

"I got it. It will be... forty-five minutes."

"Forty-five minutes? She'll be dead by then!"

"Best we can do."

"That's impossible! Please, help me. I just got here and—"

"Are you from Puerto Rico?"

She nodded and caught herself. "I was born here. After Hurricane Maria. I live in Tampa. Arrived today."

The woman on the phone sighed. "There are no stroke doctors in Puerto Rico anymore. At least not for your aunt."

A wave of nausea lurched through her. "What do you mean?"

"Unless you have a private medical provider, or the right credentials, there are no—"

"This is not happening!" she screamed. "This is not some third-world country! My titi is dying, and I'm a US citizen and—"

24

"*Nena*, we are all US citizens, but not the kind that can get this kind of medical care."

She glanced at the PASSPORT icon on her watch. The little blue dot carried far more than she expected.

"I am from the mainland. My passport is from Florida. I'm mainland American."

"Everybody says that, mija. I'm sorry, but—"

"I'm sending it to you." She tapped her wrist and confirmed the transfer on her glasses.

The wait was interminable. Back in Tampa, an emergency call would transfer all your vitals in an instant, and a doctor—real or AI—would guide you through emergency medical care until help arrived. Sending documents, encrypted or otherwise, was so commonplace that everyone had a dedicated gesture programmed into their glasses or watch. Was her island so far behind that it lacked the routine of safety and sanity of the mainland?

After a few moments, the woman on the phone interrupted her thoughts.

"Coño, you should have led with that. Someone will meet you outside in five minutes."

FIVE

SHE HAD NEVER SEEN EMTs carrying guns.

The 911 dispatcher had been wrong. Six minutes elapsed before the ambulance screeched to a halt in front of Luisa's house. The two EMTs who ran inside acted like military veterans: sharp, intense, and unwilling to waste words. Their vehicle differed from the worn-out boxes she'd seen crawling on the drive here. This ambulance looked like a delivery EV, maneuverable and fast.

"Is she on your insurance?" The male EMT, with an upturned nose and a perfect beard, glanced at Isabel as he monitored Luisa's vitals.

"I'm not—"

"You want to say yes on this one, *nena*," the female EMT whispered. "Otherwise we're going to have to leave."

"I want to say yes, but she's my aunt. I'm just visiting."

They exchanged grim stares and stared at Isabel before whispering.

"We can't take you to a unit with stroke care unless she has the right passport or the right insurance. I'm sorry."

"Okay, okay. She's with me."

The female EMT raised a doubtful eyebrow. Isabel offered her wrist, and a quick scan later, they were on their way.

Isabel couldn't see outside, but the broken pavement shook the inside of the vehicle. The air-conditioning and antiseptic tang calmed the ever-present noise and smog. The oxygen mask dug into Luisa's skin, distorting the face of a woman who had seen and survived too much.

"Everyone keeps talking about passports. What the hell is going on?"

The female EMT raised her eyebrows. "A long time ago—you were probably a little girl—our government decided they wanted special, different IDs." She adjusted the IV on Luisa and continued. "It surprised no one when they didn't meet standards. Puerto Ricans were forced to fly to the mainland with passports. Around that time, Washington decided to keep tabs on how many of us left. They started tagging our passports. Local politicians let it happen, more interested in giving out contracts to their families to issue physical IDs."

"Some cuñado made good money off the contract," the male EMT said with a derisive snort.

"What idiot allowed that to happen?"

"Fortaleza did," she replied. "All the expat money convinced them."

The male EMT chuckled and rolled his eyes.

"Yeah, but all those rich people, don't they have the same problem? Don't they have to become residents of Puerto Rico to get the tax breaks?"

The two EMTs laughed out loud.

"*Ay Bendito*, what do they tell you about us up on the mainland?"

"Nothing. You know how much the bots distort the news. I'm not sure anyone up there knows about what happens here anymore."

"You can thank the residents of Dorado for that, mija."

"There are two sets of laws in Puerto Rico," the young man said. "One for the locals, another for the expats who live here. What were you expecting?"

"I expected them to pull their weight," Isabel snapped back. "Despite the echo chambers and the misinformation, I hoped everyone would be treated fairly, have the same rights—"

"Ay Benito, nena," the man said. "No. The government gave that up when I was a baby. Depending on who you are, you have different rights and privileges."

"That's unfair. That's why we had the civil rights movement in the States."

"That will never happen here. Too much money involved."

"This is insane," Isabel replied in exasperation. "You're saying it's 'separate but equal.' The Supreme Court threw that out almost a hundred years ago!"

"It's not separate but equal, mija," the woman said. "It is separate and unequal."

SIX

"I'M SORRY. This is as far as we can take you."

Isabel nodded, breathing through her teeth. The pungent tang of disinfectant failed to mask the stench of blood and sweat. "You were wonderful. I appreciate your help."

The female EMT leaned in close. "Put her on your insurance as soon as you can. Otherwise..."

Isabel nodded again and choked back fear as they departed. She waited in a corner of the emergency room, holding her aunt's hand. Luisa, tiny and frail, seemed a whisper away from the insanity outside.

When she couldn't add Luisa onto her stateside insurance, the EMTs diverted to a local hospital. The emergency room shocked her. People with stab and gunshot wounds bled next to junkies coated in feces, shaking from withdrawal. A handful of children sat by adults shooting up in public, watching the carnage absentmindedly before returning their attention to tablets showing violent movies.

Worse of all were the old men and women, bony and frail, asleep in wheelchairs around the ER. She soon learned they'd been dropped off and abandoned, the kindest option available to desperate families unable to care for their elders. The savage decay was light years removed from the glitz of the airport, the gleaming towers in Isla Verde, and the price of everything.

She pleaded with the EMTs to take her somewhere else, anywhere. So they cut off the ingress paperwork, rolled Luisa back in the van, and drove all the way to Condado, a clinic where tourists received separate care. The EMT's left with an uncomfortable thought.

"Maybe if you... you know, pay them, they might help you with the paperwork."

She shuddered at the thought of greasing some palm to save her aunt. A clinic running on graft would be horrendous.

Her fears were allayed when she entered the triage area. This hospital was still archaic, but much improved from the carnage at Centro Médico. This facility catered to well-to-do locals and tourists, not the violent neighborhoods of San Juan. Despite the improvement, she still felt alone and afraid.

A notification on her glasses interrupted her thoughts.

MAMI

¿Como está Luisa?

She tapped the frame to compose a reply.

Bien. Estable y tranquila

When will you be back?

Not sure, when she gets better

She won't get better there.

Her mother was right. Luisa had to return home, but had to improve before a potentially fatal flight out.

An hour after an orderly moved Luisa to a waiting bed, a

young man in scrubs and a white lab coat peeked through the curtain. "Isabel Perez?"

She nodded and shook his hand.

"I'm Doctor Julián Almodovar. I'm sorry for your aunt."

Doctor Almodovar's kind eyes had seen too much. He sported a two-day growth of stubble hiding a cute dimple, and emanated resignation like mist from a lake.

"Will she be okay?"

He nodded. "I hope so. You called quickly. Probably saved her."

She took a deep breath, and sobs shuddered out.

Exhaustion descended on her. Navigating a bewildering maze in an unfamiliar home had proved frightening and shocking. Everything around her was dark and dying, wasted and faded in time. She took a halting breath between sobs and felt Doctor Almodovar's warm hand on her shoulder.

"She's going to be okay. We're going to find her the right care."

"Is she waiting on a bed?" She grimaced a tight smile.

Julián shook his head. "This hospital doesn't have a stroke ward. There are no stroke specialists in Puerto Rico. Not here, at least."

"What do you mean?" She stared at him in shock. "What happens to people when they have a stroke?"

He stood tall, looking away to hide emotion. After composing himself, he glanced back.

"They die, Isabel."

A text alert interrupted the shocking exchange. She mouthed, "I have to take this," before turning away.

PALOMA

Heard about Luisa.

Paloma, her college roommate, had returned to the island after graduation. She made it almost eighteen months, returning to

Miami in frustration and defeat. The experience had inspired Isabel to leave a promising consulting job to pursue solutions for her birthplace. They'd stayed in touch intermittently after that, their lives diverging for the past three years as each furthered their professional and personal lives. But as the maudlin cards reminded her, true friends were like stars, coming alive in the darkness.

"Hola, Paloma."

"Hey, I heard you're back on the island and your aunt is sick?"

"I'm at the hospital. They think she had an ischemic stroke."

"But we'll take care of her," Doctor Almodovar whispered. "I'll come back later."

Isabel muted her watch and dared to grab him. "Please don't leave."

He nodded and turned his attention to the antiquated monitors by Luisa's gurney.

"Hey, Paloma, can I call you back? I'm—"

"What hospital are you at?"

"Somewhere in Condado. I don't even know the name."

"I think it used to be the Ashford when we were kids. Listen, when she's set up, I'm going to have one of my friends to pick you up and—"

"Thank you, Paloma. What I may need is help with the insurance. It's crazy."

"Got it. I'll text you back. Besos."

She tapped her phone and turned. Doctor Almodovar set his tablet on Luisa's bed and crossed his arms.

"Miss Perez, there is—"

"Please, Doctor. My name is Isabel."

He paused and tried to smile. "There is no place for your aunt here."

The cold hit her first. "But I can get insurance. And I have a mainland passport. Please help her."

"Isabel." He paused and stared. "We have no stroke specialists outside Dorado. This hospital cannot provide the care your aunt needs."

Her desperation erupted in sobs. She was alone, Luisa was dying, and no one seemed able to help. Misplaced idealism had brought her home, only to see those she loved wither and fade, battling a system that no longer functioned.

Doctor Almodovar squeezed her shoulder. When their eyes met he stared into her soul, a gaze with equal measures of pain and promise. For the first time in a bewildering night, she sensed a flicker of hope.

"But I know where to find it."

SEVEN

ISABEL STARED at Julián Almodovar in shock. "She's going *where*?"

He glanced around them to ensure privacy. "I'll send the address to you. I beg you, please. Do not share this with anyone."

"Doctor, this is insane!" Isabel grabbed the bed rail to keep from falling.

"Please call me Julián," he said with a smile. "And you'll see. Por favor. *Prométemelo*."

She ventured a smile. One of the delicious differences between Spanish and English was how you could convey so much with a word. Isabel remembered a little aphorism from junior high: there are no spelling bees in Spanish, and no *novelas* in English. The right choice of words carried hidden meaning or sent pointed messages.

Prométemelo. Promise me, in the informal. No *Please promise me, Miss Perez*. This was close and comfortable. *Promise me, Isabel*.

She had no intention of breaking his trust.

"*Te lo prometo*." A volley back. No *Of course, Doctor*, but a whisper heavy with meaning. *I promise you*.

She felt her cheeks flush. Her aunt lay unconscious in a

hospital bed, and she was distracted by a cutie in scrubs. She needed to be strong, focused, and ruthless—not a chatty teenager with a crush.

Julián tapped on his wrist. "I sent it. Can I have your info?" He caught himself. "To follow up."

"Of course."

One tap later, he nodded. "Great. Do you have a ride?"

"Don't you have an ambulance?"

He shook his head. "Not for where she's going."

"I think I can call someone."

"Can you trust them?"

She nodded. "My friend Paloma can find someone?"

He shook his head. "I'm sorry, I can't."

"Well, the guy who picked me up at the airport? He seemed very put together. Military guy."

Julián raised an eyebrow. "Do you have his information?"

"Yeah. He gave me his info in case I needed help." She flipped through her transactions and found him. "Here."

Julián tapped on his watch and smiled. "You met Roberto. Perfect."

"You know him?"

"I do. Hope he wasn't hitting on you."

For an instant, she wanted to reply with a flirty "maybe."

"How do you know him?"

He stared at the wall before replying. "Let's just say we have a lot in common."

EIGHT

"THIS IS PRETTY FAR AWAY," Isabel said and glanced down at Luisa, laying quiet by her side.

"We're headed to Bayamón," Roberto said, glancing in the rear-view mirror. "Just a little further."

Isabel was worried the driver might not remember her when she called him direct, but Roberto was very kind. "La gringa de Cupey," he teased.

Then she brought up Doctor Julián. The change in his voice was immediate.

"I'll be there in five minutes."

He made it in eight, which, given the state of the roads and traffic on her beautiful island, was insanely fast. Julián—no longer Doctor Almodovar—asked an orderly to wheel Luisa out a back entrance, which Isabel later found out was only used by funeral homes. Julián and Roberto shook hands through a close hug. Deep friendship ran beneath the gesture. They parted with a knowing nod, which said everything.

Roberto reconfigured the inside of the enormous EV in seconds. He pulled out a little box which measured vital signs and connected a hose to Luisa's oxygen mask. Isabel had seen these devices in news holos—oxygen on demand, using some kind of solid-state electrolysis. In the field, hydrogen was diverted to fuel cells, the excess vented off. The device keeping Luisa stable was the same gear used to treat the injured in the wars in Azerbaijan, Belarus, and Georgia.

"How'd you get this?" He met her question with icy silence. She stayed quiet until the dark roads turned into an urban landscape reminiscent of Tampa's better quarters.

"Where are we?"

"The metropolis of Bayamón," he said, and she didn't know if he was kidding. "They run things differently. Sit back. We may have a bit of a wait."

She was about to ask why, when they slowed down for red lights glinting in the intermittent mist. They queued up behind several cars lined at what reminded Isabel of a checkpoint from a 2020s movie.

They crept up to a policeman equipped with body armor, tactical communications gear, and an assault rifle. Had his uniform been green or tan, he would've passed for a soldier stationed in the Middle East. Roberto lowered the window. The humidity and stench of garbage and smoke shocked her.

"¿A donde se dirige?" the man asked. Roberto tapped the center console on the car, then waved his watch. The young man tapped on something familiar—a display mounted on a forearm—and checked something on the tiny screen. After an instant, he glared at her and Luisa. Isabel's heart stopped—had they been found?

But the policeman motioned them through. Huge metal spikes, a barrier invisible until now, retracted into the pavement, and they drove past.

They entered the first world. Gleaming buildings loomed ahead. Compact cars—instead of bodies—lined streets glistening from rain. As they neared the city, she recognized familiar shops and stores. Everything was clean and neat.

"Well, this is a little different."

"Bayamón is one of the few municipalities with money," Roberto replied.

"Taxes?"

"Not on people. Businesses. But they get what they pay for."

"More bribery, I imagine?"

He shook his head. "Puerto Rico has more municipalities than the mainland has states. They're all tiny, so they rely on some ridiculous agreement where the government levies taxes and the cities get a cut." Roberto waved his hand at the idea. "Of course, it hasn't worked that way for a hundred years. The politicians keep the money for bullshit contracts to their families."

"That seems to be the only topic of conversation on this island."

He chuckled at her through the rear-view mirror. "Politics. Our favorite sport."

They drove through tidy commercial parks, glistening dark in the humid night. For the first time, she noticed overlays on her glasses. These business—bakeries, nail salons, pet stores—had the same digital presence as any other shop back in Tampa. She realized with a start that she'd yet to see any of that on the island. As if time had stopped early in the century, and the world had moved on. Bayamón seemed the exception.

"Why does this place look so different?"

"A decade ago, the mayor told the government, 'Go to hell,' and they now run their own show. Now it is the safest and fastest growing municipality. One of a handful of places where locals can live and make clean money."

They entered the outskirts of the city, leaving the boulevard behind. Here streetlights pointed down, not up—a sign of enlightened design. Urban governments long ago realized they could save energy and attract tourists by preserving the night sky. Even Florida, after some disastrous administrations focused more on culture wars than citizen welfare, had acknowledged that on a planet of ten billion people, humans longed for the wild.

Despite the lights, pedestrian streets, and cleanliness, Bayamón was not perfect. Roberto drove until they reached a decrepit and forgotten neighborhood a few blocks from the city center. He pulled into an alley, and once again, Isabel's heart sank.

"Please tell me you're not going to hurt us," she whispered.

Roberto stopped the car, mashed the button for the parking brake, and turned to her.

"For whatever reason, you're friends with Julián Almodovar," he said through clenched teeth. "Consider yourself fortunate."

NINE

ISABEL HELD her aunt's hand—warmer now—and swallowed.

"What's next?"

"We wait."

"We wait? While someone needs—"

"Doctor Almodovar has put a lot on the line for you, Señorita Perez. Don't push your luck."

She was about to reply with something impolite when Roberto flashed her a thumbs up. He stepped out of the car and motioned her to follow.

"What about Titi Luisa?"

"You want help? Come with me."

"But she'll be out here all alone and—"

He stepped close enough for him to feel fear.

"Your aunt is in the second safest place on this island. My car," he hissed. "The safest is in there." He motioned an impatient thumb at a green metal door, covered in rust, with a decrepit pad at chest height.

He turned without a word, and the SUV locked behind them. The night was heavy and wet, the silence ringing in her ears.

Roberto waved his watch at a cheesy doorbell that had been obsolete ten years before all personal information had migrated onto smartwatches. She was wondering what Roberto's problem might be when the door clicked open.

"After you. Quickly."

She entered a poorly lit foyer, with black and white linoleum tile, a puke green couch on the corner, and a metal door on the far end. The door to the outside—to Luisa, to Bayamón, to Puerto Rico—closed, and on cue, a thin man entered the room.

He reminded Isabel of Julián Almodovar, if Julián had been cruel, a criminal, and a sociopath. No kindness sparked from his eyes. For an instant, Isabel wondered if Roberto had taken her to a drug dealer—or a riñonero.

"Let me read your insurance," the man said. No "hello," no introductions, nothing.

She raised her hand, and he waved a small tablet close to it. The man turned, paging through Isabel's information. An amber light pulsed in her glasses, a warning the man had downloaded much of her personal information. She tapped her glasses, trying to determine what the man now possessed.

The answer: everything.

She tried to recall the sequence for undoing a transaction when the man interrupted her.

"Distributed ledger. You can't undo it. Don't worry." He stared without a smile. "We do this a lot."

She was about to reply when the man shook his head.

"Sorry. Can't do it."

"What do you mean, you can't do it?" she demanded.

"I mean," he said, stepping closer, "that your insurance is no good. Might work in Florida, but not here. Your aunt is no better. Can't do it."

"I still don't understand. Why can't you help?"

He sneered at the audacity of someone doubting him. "Your aunt had an ischemic stroke. Still don't know if it will hemorrhage. We're the only people for a hundred miles who can fix it." He looked her up, as if inspecting meat. "But I don't like your attitude. You're probably some *vende patria* who left when shit went south and—"

"I am not giving up!" She shook with rage. "Do not ever accuse me of giving up. I left as a baby, but I'm back, unlike many others. Don't you dare lecture me on my birthplace!"

"Ooh, a feisty one," the man said with a sneer before leaning closer. "We don't work for free, *princesa*. So if you can't pay—"

"I will do anything to help her," she hissed back. "Please. Por amor a Dios, ayúdenme."

"You'd do anything?"

She froze, a breath away from selling herself to save her aunt.

"I would," she whispered and swallowed her shame.

The man stopped, changing before her eyes. Gone was the arrogance, the veiled violence, the hate. He tilted his head and flashed a kind smile. In one sigh, the asshole vanished, replaced with someone who understood.

He held up a tablet with her information. "These things don't tell us everything. Sometimes we have to make sure. You're safe."

Roberto touched her arm. "I'm gonna go bring her in. Stay here."

He walked out, leaving her alone with the madman.

"My name is Federico Velazquez," he said. "Sorry for the drama."

"I'm Isabel." Her mind reeled at the change in the man's demeanor, something he wore like armor. "Do you do that to everyone?"

"Julián Almodovar is my best friend," he said with a wink. "You got off easy."

45

The outside door opened, and Roberto wheeled Luisa in on a strange black gurney.

Federico tapped his earbud. "Let's prep her for surgery."

"Are you the surgeon?"

"No. I'm the anesthesiologist. But my friend in Barcelona is the absolute shit."

TEN

THEY WHEELED Titi Luisa through the crappy foyer on the weirdest gurney Isabel had ever seen. The device was spindly, with matte black arms extending from a lattice basket to the ground. Small wheels shod in chunky tires glided over the uneven tile floor. The contraption looked like it could hold ten men and probably weighed less than her tablet.

"Don't tell me." She pointed at the device. "More soldier goodies?"

"Don't ask, don't tell," Roberto replied with a wink.

Federico tapped open the door and they entered a spacious medical office. In one corner, behind cloth sheeting, a medical robot stood unmoving beside a hospital bed. Across from it, a handful of people in scrubs tended to a desk overflowing with monitors. Beyond them, a shuttered room. Across from that, more doors. The antiseptic tang of cleanliness felt comfortable, despite the chill.

"What is this?"

"This is the best hospital in Puerto Rico," Roberto answered. "Except it doesn't exist."

The monitors to her right glowed with information: an image from Luisa's personal documentation, EKG traces, video feeds of a man wearing an AR headset conversing with the people in the room.

"Telemedicine?"

Federico nodded. "Illegal as sin. Unless you're an expat in Dorado."

She looked at him, confused. "Telemedicine is illegal here?"

He laughed. "I forget you're not from here. If you have a local passport—" He was about to ask if she knew about them, and Isabel nodded. "If you're a local, you have to be on local insurance. And that won't pay for the latest technology. Fortaleza doesn't allow it." He made air quotes and sneered. "It takes business away from the local doctors and is 'unfair.' Otherwise, they'd leave."

"But they left anyway," she replied.

"Of course they did! The government also put a cap on how many patients they could see, imposed a bunch of paperwork, and instituted a ceiling on billing. They legislated how much a doctor could make."

She stopped, mouth agape.

"But if you're a mainlander living in Dorado, or Palmas, or Aguadilla…" He waved his arms around him in a sign of cynical extravagance. "Well, then, we don't want you 'taking' medical care from the locals. So you can bring your own. The expats don't have to mingle with locals or their pesky regulations." He snapped his fingers. "Voila!"

"Medical tourism," she muttered.

Federico nodded. "The largest such industry on the planet. As long as you're not from here."

"That is insane! Even with all the doctors leaving Puerto Rico?"

Federico nodded. "They have been for decades. The only lucrative job left is being a lawyer for the expats." He flashed a wicked smile. "Or a consultant for Fortaleza."

She shook her head in disbelief as a handful of techs in scrubs took Luisa behind the plastic sheet. "This island is not working. And every time I ask why, people tell me the politicians did it. How can they be so shortsighted?" She waved her arms. "There's no medical care, no security. Don't they know that what they're doing is killing the island?"

"It's not all bad," he replied with a wink. "We have the third-biggest black market for kidneys in the Caribbean!"

"That's not helping," she said, and Roberto laughed.

"You forgot there's also no public education." Federico scribbled frantic notes on a tablet. "They know they're killing us. But to their credit, it is damn hard to make good decisions when you make minimum wage as a public servant, and some trust fund donor offers you a life of riches."

"Come on. How can the political class be paid minimum wage?" Her frustration rose with the volume of her voice.

"Because that is the best way to control them."

ELEVEN

"YOU'LL WANT to sit back here," Federico said. "Need anything?"

Isabel shook her head. "Is she okay?"

"She'll be fine," Roberto said. He seemed to dress for combat: tactical boots, an ankle holster, various devices hanging from straps on his thighs and belt. He still wore his body armor, loosening the straps as a minor concession for comfort. She noticed other things, too: a scar on his chin, calloused hands, and a permanent scowl.

"We'll come get you when we're done." Federico tapped something on his tablet. An instant later, an acknowledgement popped on Isabel's glasses.

"You did it."

Federico nodded. "Yep. You, Isabel Maria Perez, now have a dependent, covered under your insurance. As of..." He glanced at his watch and beamed at her. "About four minutes ago." He leaned in for a theatrical whisper. "Someone in some insurance company must like your friend Paloma a lot."

"Oh god..." Her breath came out in a laugh and a sob. "Oh, my god. I cannot thank you enough... oh, thank you—"

"Thank Paloma and your friend Julián," he said with a wink and tapped his watch. "Doc is logging in. Gotta go."

She peeked out the window as he entered the central room. Screens around Titi Luisa's prone figure lit up with faces, charts, and diagrams. The medical robot beeped to life, a rainbow of diagnostics lighting up in complex test patterns. The setup for surgery rivaled any she'd seen in Tampa.

She turned from the scene, fighting emotion. It was late, and the day's wild ride was not over. But by all accounts, Luisa appeared to be in good hands—the best outcome from what she'd seen during a bewildering day. Despite everything broken around them, people were still good. They took care of each other—of her —in the most impossible circumstances. She wiped her eyes and flashed a thin smile at Roberto.

"Thank you for staying," she whispered.

He waved off the offer of friendship.

"I mean it. You didn't have to."

He closed his book—no magazines in this waiting room, only hardcovers which felt a hundred years old—and leaned forward, elbows on his knees.

"Can we get some fresh air?"

"You don't need to be walking alone at night."

"Would you go with me?"

His face hardened as he clenched his jaw. "I'm tired."

"I can fend for myself?"

"Not here."

"But we're in Bayamón," she said with a playful smile.

"Even in Bayamón," he replied.

"Can I ask why you're so serious?"

Time stopped. Roberto stared at her with a blank expression.

"You remind me of my sister."

"Then she must be awesome," she said with a grin.

"You're the same age she was when she was murdered. She thought she was pretty tough too."

A shard of ice ripped through her. "I—I am so sorry. I didn't mean to—"

"She was visiting, like you. Some brewery in Condado. Bunch of mules decided to race their Lambos on a two-lane street. One ran over her friend. The second one shot my sister when she tried to help."

"Dios mío." She stared at the linoleum and shook.

"She didn't know about riñoneros, or corruption, or the laws that perpetuate poverty for two-thirds of our island." His voice rasped with resignation and anger. "She just wanted to finish nursing school in Charlotte. Came here to have a good time. Spring break with her friends."

He stood up, placed the book on the table, and stared at the wall. "We couldn't bear to bury her here. I flew back to North Carolina with her ashes."

"Why are you still here?"

He turned to her, his jaw rippling with hate. "Because one day, those *hijoeputas* will need a ride, and I'll be there. And it will be the last ride of their lives."

She wanted to answer something, anything. That revenge was a cancer, that walking away was the only wise option, that taking someone's life was never the solution to any problem. But she couldn't. She could not fathom the anger, the emptiness of losing a family member under such horrific circumstances, then having to face the same injustice day after day.

"I'm so sorry," she said instead. "I cannot imagine how you feel."

He stared for a while before wiping emotion from his eyes. "You even sound like her."

TWELVE

SHE STARTLED awake to find Federico's eyes boring into her.

"You up?"

She nodded and wiped her mouth out of habit, hoping she hadn't drooled.

"What time is it?"

"About three in the morning," Federico said and stretched. "Quitting time in Barcelona."

"How is she?"

He shrugged. "She's stable. Glad we went in. Bahamontes found some vascularity at risk of rupture." He stared at Isabel and understood she had captured none of that. "He took care of this stroke and made sure she doesn't have another one."

"Will she make it?"

"Let's put it this way. We're all gonna die. She will too, but not of a stroke."

Isabel laughed. Federico had the worst, or perhaps best, bedside manner of anyone she'd met. She lunged and pulled him in for a hug.

"Hey, don't thank me. I just put her to sleep."

She tried to appear insulted, but smiled instead.

"Doc wants to speak to you. Got a few minutes?"

"Claro que sí."

He placed a finger to his lips and opened the door into the central area. Roberto lay on the couch, on edge even as he slept.

A tech in purple scrubs showed her to a screen glowing with the image of a man in a collared shirt.

"Are you the patient's guardian?" The man spoke in a thick Iberian accent.

"Si. I'm her niece."

"Bien. Doña Luisa had an ischemic stroke. Imaging showed a high risk for a hemorrhagic episode in the future. We treated the ischemic lesion and repaired the site of the vascular defect."

Little of this made sense, but Federico had already explained her outcome.

"What's the prognosis?"

"Did Doctor Velazquez tell you?" It took her a moment to realize he was talking about Federico. She smiled and nodded.

"Wish I could see your real face right now, but the prognosis is good."

She let out a deep sigh, then paused. "What do you mean, my real face?"

He broke into a warm smile. "I don't want to go to jail. Neither do you."

"Who are you?"

"Don't ask, don't tell."

"But you have all my information. What if—"

He raised a hand. "Quantum encryption. NATO grade. Your information is safe. But humans remember faces. Unless they're fake."

"You're not some dude from Barcelona?"

The man laughed. "I'm not even a man."

"How can I ever thank you? You've saved her life. You and this team worked a miracle, and—"

"Don't thank me," he said. "Tell Doctor Almodovar we said hi."

The image faded to a point, then black. Federico—Doctor Velazquez—tapped a sequence of keys.

"And... there you go. Another conversation that never happened."

"You guys go through a lot of trouble staying anonymous."

"Don't want the government to shut us down because we're doing the right thing."

"What you do here is amazing."

"Some people go through entire lives searching for meaning," Federico said. "We don't have that problem."

"What's next for her? When do I take her?"

"We had to sedate her for the microsurgery. The robot is awesome, but we're still going into the cranium through blood vessels. So Doña Luisa will be with us for a couple of days. She needs to heal under observation and with minimal disruption."

"Where? Here?"

Federico gestured over his shoulder. "Back there. Through the green door."

A set of doors behind him led further into the building. The cobwebs of fatigue cleared, and Isabel understood. Whoever had built this clinic had thought of everything.

"Get some rest. I'll reconnect with you tomorrow. Where are you staying?"

"I don't know. I was going to stay with her in Cupey."

"Cupey? I don't think so."

He tapped the shoulder of the young woman in purple scrubs. She blinked at her glasses, then swept information onto a monitor.

"We should have space in one of the attendant apartments." The girl tapped the screen, and flashed Federico a thumbs-up.

"Where is it?"

"Condado. She'll send you the pin."

Isabel blinked to accept the address, nodding a "thank you" at the girl. She tiptoed into the waiting room: Roberto was the last person on Earth she'd want to startle. He must've sensed her closing the door and rustled awake.

"Hey." He slurred his words as he tried to open his eyes. "How's your Titi?"

"Fede told me she's out of the woods. Thank you."

"I didn't do shit," he said through a yawn. "I'm just the driver."

"I would've never made it here without you." She tackled him in an awkward hug. Metal and straps and rough nylon poked at her. She did not mind.

He squeezed his eyes to clear away fatigue and nodded a tired smile. "I'll take that."

THIRTEEN

THE DRIVE to the hotel reminded her of a nightmare where every path leads to peril. At four in the morning, that empty time which the ignorant consider safe, the island seethed. Cars in every shape imaginable—some still powered by gas—raced across the freeways, ignoring safety and common sense. The neighborhoods outside Condado rose out of some apocalyptic movie, the houses demolished and unrecognizable through rubble and graffiti. A handful of people walked the sidewalks, ignoring the devastation, illuminated by feeble streetlights flickering from a wobbly power grid shaky from decades of neglect.

Then everything changed. Blocks from the hotel, the island's chaos slammed shut. The rubble and pockmarked streets gave way to worn sidewalks, manicured hedges, and high walls surrounding the gleaming apartment buildings that dominated the night. The hotel rose in a column of steel and glass wedged among renovated apartments from the middle of the last century. She hadn't seen anything this trendy in years.

"I could use a night in a place like this," Roberto said as he stopped the car.

Isabel smiled. "Where do you live?"

He craned his neck and pointed past the Condado Lagoon. "Can't see it from here. High rise in Hato Rey. Only thirty years old or so. Nice, but not as nice as this."

"It's close, though. That's gotta help."

"I might as well be on the other side of the world."

Roberto insisted on dropping her off at the front and helping her with the luggage. She dared to hug him before he walked away, smiling when he returned the gesture. She waved as the black SUV wheeled into the dawn, leaving her alone in a bright lobby ripe with the scent of expensive bath concoctions.

"Buenas noches." The young woman sounded chipper for this early in the morning. "O Buenos Dias." She gestured at the pad for her watch, standard fare for checking into hotels on the mainland. Isabel realized this was the first such device she'd seen in a bewildering day. The first two hospitals where Roberto took her were far less equipped than a simple hotel.

She waved her watch, and the attendant tapped her tablet. "Isabel? You're in Room 1050. Just sent you the key. Mister..." she tilted her head and smiled. "Fortunato Vizcarrondo. Like the poet. He's set you up."

She nodded in response, grabbed her bag, and beelined for the elevators.

A short ride later, she entered a room straight from a Nordic furniture store. The chest of drawers and bed—clean and bright— were simple, utilitarian, and elegant. Minimalist art complemented the off-white walls, and the comforting aroma of expensive bath soaps suffused the crisp air. The floor to ceiling window, the first one she'd seen without bars interrupting the view, looked out onto Miramar, Tras Talleres, and beyond.

She opened the glass and stepped onto the balcony. The upper floors of the hotel provided some escape from the stench of smoke and garbage ever-present at street level. Shots, sirens, and the buzz of generators fought for attention as an orange wisp of dawn pushed against the blackness. Pools of dark bloomed among the constellation of streetlights beyond Miramar, and she wondered what those lives might yearn for. The black pockets of emptiness pierced through Barrio Obrero, Hato Rey, and Cataño. Twenty-five years after Hurricane Maria, too many still lived in darkness.

She closed the balcony glass, shutting out the noise and smoke and heat behind her, feeling guilty for her current fortune. Unbelievable stories about the island now failed to convey the situation. In one day, the worst of the rumors had proven true: the island boiled in a stew of smoke and garbage, crime was rampant, inequality permeated everything, and everyone lived in extremes.

But there were bright lights among the despair. Doctor Julián Almodovar, Federico Velazquez, Roberto, the driver. She tapped her glasses to record a message for Julián.

"Thank you for helping me today. You've been a ray of sunshine in the darkness. I'm in your debt."

She thought of Titi Luisa recovering alone, spending the night somewhere she'd never expected. Isabel plopped on the bed—soft, welcoming, comfortable—a gentle solace before her emotions rushed out.

In seconds, she was asleep.

FOURTEEN

ISABEL OPENED her eyes to the vibration on her watch.

She bolted upright and touched her face. Her glasses! She fumbled around in confusion until she realized she could answer from her watch.

JULIÁN ALMODOVAR

"Uh, hullo?"

"Buenos días, Isabel. Did I wake you?"

"No. Not at all. Of course not." She rubbed her eyes, thankful that Julián could not see her in this state.

He chuckled at the lie. "Thanks for your message. I heard your aunt is doing well."

"She is. I cannot thank you enough. I'd love to buy you dinner, or whatever you want. That was—"

"I'll settle for a coffee."

She was now wide awake. "It is—" her mouth dropped when she saw the time. "Dios mio, it is ten o'clock. Is it too late?"

She liked the sound of his laugh. "Isabel, por favor! There's always time for coffee. There's a great shop next door from your hotel. Meet you in half an hour?"

She nodded and followed up with a soft "yes."

"Nos vemos."

Half an hour. She stood up to catch her reflection on the balcony window and stopped cold.

She'd never seen El Condado during the day. The room, ten floors above street level, peered south toward La Placita, Santurce, and Hato Rey. Far beyond, the exurbia of Rio Piedras, Carolina, and Bayamón, blurry through the haze.

The streets below seemed pulled out of Miami. Shiny EVs—too many of them choking the roads—inched their way through traffic in a cacophonous fugue of honks and yells. The few people walking the streets yelled at unseen callers through their glasses, watches, and sometimes even phones. But only a few blocks away, the gleaming buildings gave way to decay. Walls of graffiti ten stories high rose around snapped wooden posts with tangled nests of wires blocking the view, something Isabel had only seen in reels of third-world countries. She opened the window to peek outside, and an oily hum assaulted her. The smoke of something sweet, oily, and rotten hung in the air.

She shut the smell away. Thousands of cars blasting through the island still ran on gasoline. Uncountable generators provided a lifeline to people living without electricity. The power keeping her cool and isolated from the decay outside came not from the sun, but from oil.

She reeled at the insanity. Families still burned fuel for electricity! Cables strung above ground sagged close to the pavement, a dangerous setup she hadn't seen for years. Streets pockmarked with potholes the size of craters swallowed cars and debris. Garbage stuck to plants growing everywhere. Smoke from unseen piles of smoldering debris rose in gray ribbons before being swept by the ocean's breeze.

None of this made the feeds on the mainland. The slick tourism holos never showed the extent of the rot and decay. Anyone watching those would imagine her island as a paradise. The reasons for the discrepancy between propaganda and reality she knew well. In a world of manufactured facts, keeping this decay hidden was less conspiracy than accident: a consequence of manipulated attention, and lack of focus. Finding the truth was possible only by overcoming the brutal curation of algorithms designed to distract, monetize, and forget. The world had to be experienced first-hand, a self-referential truism somehow lost in the mid-21st century. Whether by accident or on purpose, the reality of her beautiful island had been forgotten and misplaced. Few knew the truth, and even less cared.

But she wouldn't forget. She tapped her glasses to record a voice memo.

"I'm awake, after a bewildering few hours. My trip here started with someone trying to take my kidney, huddling under a rain of bullets, and almost losing my aunt. It ended with me finding a pirate medical clinic and staying in a hotel that reminds me of a spaceship on a hostile planet. I've seen death and destruction meters away from overbearing opulence. And it is only night one."

She took a deep breath and continued. "But I've been privileged to meet noble people. Doctors who risk everything to treat the sick. A former soldier who cannot forget. EMTs dedicated to erasing the pain of others. Our island may be hurting, but our people are strong. It makes me so proud."She wiped a tear, surprised at the emotion.

She finished the recording and raced to prepare for her date with Julián. The shower—bright and smart—stuck out of place after what she'd seen from her lofty perch. Everything was in tension—insane riches existing feet from deep poverty. How both existed without a spark verged on impossible.

She toweled her hair, pulled on some travel pants and a blouse, and stopped. This would not do.

She blew her hair upside down to give it some lift, applied her favorite lip gloss and mascara, and picked the cutest dress in her bag before striding out with a satisfied smile.

She wondered what Doctor Julián Almodovar would look like without scrubs.

FIFTEEN

THE TRANSITION from hotel lobby to street reminded her of an airlock. On one side, cool air, the latest scents, and cutting-edge electronica. Outside, blasting heat, cracked sidewalks and pavement, the affront of smoke and fire and decay. The buzz of the city —cars honking insults, generators belching smoke, and the incessant roar of trucks—shredded the silence. Behind it all, something lovely: the scent of coffee and bread, the soft cooing of pigeons in the late morning heat, and the gentle roar of the sea. Despite everything, she was home.

She glanced back at the hotel, to the chilly foyer three feet behind her and a world away, and shook her head. The island existed in contrast.

Julián was right—the cafe was steps away, next door to the hotel. This was one of the many things she loved about her home: it was impossible to find a bakery separated from a coffee shop. She walked into the cool, dark bakery, anticipating the simple pleasures she'd longed for during her trip.

"Isabel?"

Julián dazzled her with soft eyes and a bright smile. She was glad he hadn't shaved. He wore a long sleeve linen shirt, pale blue shorts, and canvas shoes. On anyone else, the outfit would've marked them as a tourist. He looked like a model.

He offered his hand, which she took for a respectful moment before pulling him into a hug, enveloped in his oaky scent. For the first time in too long, she felt safe.

"Thank you so much for—" she stopped talking before emotion betrayed her.

She did not mind when he held on and let her cry. After a bit, she stepped back and wiped her eyes. "I'm so sorry. I imagine you get that from everyone."

"Actually, I don't. Thank you."

They ordered coffee—she had the same cortado as him, with a quesito and an empanadilla on the side. They sat in a corner, vacated moments earlier by a dreadlocked couple with a Boston accent.

"I heard Luisa is doing well."

"I got a message from Federico. Doctor Velazquez, I mean."

He leaned forward and shot an uncomfortable glance that screamed, *not here.*

"I'm sorry," she whispered. "Did I say something wrong?"

"So, where did you go to school?" He tried to smile while changing the subject. "You never told me."

She sat up, following his lead. "UF. Harvard of the South. I'll start a master's at UNC this fall. Human-machine policy."

"Chapel Hill? I did a residency at Wake Forest."

"No way! How was it?"

He stared at her. "I missed home."

"Is that why you came back?"

He nodded. "I made a commitment."

All warmth left her. Of course he would. She tried to smile, feeling pathetic for allowing herself a fleeting fantasy with this kind and beautiful man.

"Are they..."

He shook his head. "Not like that. My commitment is here. To the island."

The cafe brightened, and the air tasted sweet. "Tell me more."

"Not much to tell. I saw how perfect everything was in North Carolina, and I wanted to bring it back."

"What did you find?"

He turned away, looking outside, lost in thought. "Our people don't deserve this. I wanted to do my part."

She leaned to look past him and realized the hospital she'd first taken Luisa was across the street. "You're serving your island. Our island. I think that is the most noble thing we can do. I left as a baby and still think I need to do more."

"More of us out there than here," he said with a wink. "And the way the news works now, they don't always find out what is really happening to their home. Unless you work at it, the news gets lost in the algorithms."

"My mom said that when she was young, she could listen to Puerto Rican radio stations on the phone. They had real reporters, not the AI bots dishing out whatever the owners want you to hear."

"Remember those super loud traffic and weather segments? My mom would race to the TV every time to turn them down."

"What?" Isabel said. "I can't hear you!"

They chuckled like kids at the shared memory. She wanted to talk with him for hours.

"After this trip, I think the policy impact of information over-load is going to be my dissertation in grad school. The whole 'make up your own newsfeed' is hiding a lot of economic damage."

He nodded. "Gets worse every year. That's why I have two jobs."

She sat up in shock. "You have to work another job? As a doctor?"

"Not exactly. I work in two clinics."

"Isn't that common?"

He winced. "Sort of."

"Where's the other one?"

"Dorado."

She froze. "God no."

"What's wrong?"

She glared at him, hurt beyond anything she could explain.

"So you're a personal doctor to some crypto cowboy or some hedge fund billionaire?"

"No. My practice—"

"Who gets most of your attention, Julián? Us? Or the expats who are destroying our island?"

She wanted to snap at him. The Puerto Rican diaspora might not be a united front, but they unanimously despised one "feature" emerging from the excesses of the island's tax haven: expat millionaires insisting on separate medical care.

What started out as tax breaks decades ago had metastasized into something from a horror movie. Rich foreigners in Puerto Rico had access to every miracle of modern medical science. None of it was shared with the locals, who would die before receiving life-saving treatment at the bastions of the ultra-rich. The Hippocratic oath applied to every physician on the planet, but was imprisoned inside the gated communities of Dorado, Palmas, and Aguadilla.

When she first heard about such injustice, she'd smoldered in rage. Last night she lived it with her aunt. Now she sat with someone who enabled it.

Julián must've sensed her disgust. "Do you want to go for a walk?"

"It's a hundred and ten out there, Julián. Where are we going? A swanky hotel owned by your 'patients?'"

He was no longer the object of a budding crush. Before her eyes he'd turned into the worst of the island: the locals who served the predators who pilfered and raped Borinquen for their own, the traitors who facilitated the economic slavery that fated the middle class to failure, the poor to violence and pestilence. All for a chance to fight for the scraps of money the billionaires dropped on the floor.

She'd raced from smitten to disgusted in an instant.

"I have a lot to tell you." He stood up and held out his hand. "Please."

She paused long enough to let him know she hated him, then walked out into the hell of the midday sun.

SIXTEEN

"WHY ARE WE HERE?"

Isabel stared out into the Atlantic Ocean, blue and endless and wild. They'd walked out of the cafe, made it a block in the stifling heat and stench of garbage. They escaped the sticky blast furnace, scurrying into the hotel lobby and savoring the sweet, cool air. She was torn between hating Julián and wanting to know more. She found a hat to survive the onslaught of the sun, and, still angry, met him at the hotel's rooftop.

Tourists covered in sunscreen lounged by a pool which Isabel imagined must be refrigerated, lest they scald themselves in the water. Puerto Rico boiled in defiance of a burning planet. While the world suffered the worst climate calamities in millennia, her island still imported oil to burn.

She followed the seawall far below them, avoiding Julián's gaze. The structure tucked in and out of the waves, protecting wide stretches of hotel beaches, then veering inland to hold entire buildings against the raging sea. The system reminded her of a scaled-down version of what Tampa had installed to save the historic downtown districts from the rising bay.

Last night at the clinic, Roberto had shared how bad the past decade had been for the island. The rising sea had long ago swallowed the historic beaches of Piñones and Luquillo. Many other beaches across Puerto Rico, those not protected by mangroves, suffered similar fate. The enclaves of the rich were the unsurprising exception. Somehow, the government found money, new sand, and construction firms to protect the villas in Dorado and Palmas from the onslaught. They rationalized the injustice by claiming the loss of tourism revenue. But the expense of rescuing opulent communities plunged the island deeper into debt. The vanishing middle class would never be able to pay any of it back. Puerto Rico was a paradise only for those not born here, paid for by those who were.

Julián's touch on her arm brought her back to the moment. "Isabel, please. Can we talk?"

She grabbed her hat against the scorching breeze. "I can't believe you didn't tell me you were a leech."

"That's not what I said."

She despised him enough to wish he'd never say her name again. "So, what's your excuse?"

He glanced around them, preparing to share a secret. "How do you think I fund it?"

"Fund what? Your nice car? Your boat? What?"

He pulled her in for a whisper. "The clinic."

Her shield cracked. "That's... you? You built that?"

He nodded. "Someone had to."

The shame in his eyes stopped her breath.

"Dios mio." She squeezed his hand. "I'm sorry."

"I couldn't stand to live in a place where medical care is 'separate but unequal.' So I did something. Fede was my classmate." He glanced around, hiding their conversation from the bored tourists. "We met the Spanish docs at a medical conference. Decided to use the same telemedicine technology they use in the Sahel. We save lives, Isabel. A lot of lives. And I can do it because..."

His nostrils flared as he gazed out to sea. "Because I sold my soul to the rich."

"Doctor Almodovar, I'm so sorry, I—"

"¡Por Dios, Isabel! My name is Julián."

Her name sounded beautiful when he said it. "Discúlpame, Julián."

"This has been my life. I live in two worlds." He breathed in the hot ocean air. "The expats still deserve care, of course. But they have the ailments of the rich. Cancer, and diabetes, and Alzheimer's. Also their share of domestic violence, substance abuse, and STDs. Not to mention screening for all sorts of plastic surgery and augmentation."

He sneered at the last one. She held the brim of her hat and looked around her. Every woman sunning by the pool showed the unmistakable signs of plastic surgery. Most of the men had the too-dark hair, red skin, and out-of-place musculature of cheap gene therapy. None of them were locals.

"And then I come back there." He pointed to the hospital across the street. Ancient air-conditioning units hung from windows by the barest of rusted straps. Peeling paint flaked from deep cracks in the salt-blasted concrete. The hospital seemed a universe away from the meticulous and trendy setting of the hotel pool. "And I treat the diseases of the poor, of the struggling, with equipment from the turn of the century. Mental health and gunshots. Exhaustion and malnutrition. I had a patient with scurvy. Scurvy, in the 2040s, on an island that still ships in food. Can you believe that?" He shook his head and grimaced. "Do you know that we haven't had a stroke specialist in San Juan since you were a teenager? But five live in one compound in Dorado. And they won't treat patients from the island."

She caught her breath and looked down at the streets. A lone figure, wearing an oversized hat to stave off the sun, pushed something in front of a parking lacking solar collectors. The temperature inside the parked cars would be enough to cook meat, yet no one harvested the sunlight turning them to ovens. Whoever walked the hellscape of the sidewalks below was clearly homeless, light-years removed from the blithe, overweight tourists drinking themselves numb in the blazing heat. She winced at the disparity between the damned and the entitled.

"How can this happen?"

His jaw shook with rage. "Bureaucracy. Years ago, the government tried to ensure people were,"—he made the gesture for quotes—"certified. The requirements became a joke: a journey of red tape impossible to navigate. Unless you paid the right people." He swung his hand around him. "Like everything else here. That's how the politicians fund their lifestyles. Paying to overcome red tape is the easiest way for the government to make money."

"Aren't there other doctors in Dorado?"

"They don't fall under our rules," he said with a sneer. "Once the government started allowing foreign investors to not pay taxes, they started demanding a lot. They insisted that they be allowed to have their own medical care, or they'd take their money. The government caved. Their only request was that those doctors don't treat any of the locals."

"Why not?"

"If the system works, no one gets paid under the table."

A wave of nausea almost doubled her over. "Is it that bad?"

"I couldn't stand by and live with that. So I had to become part of the problem to fix it. Their medical personnel can't treat Puerto Ricans. There's nothing to say that a Puerto Rican doctor can't care for them. Yale Med School was my ticket in."

He tried to smile through shame. "Now you know."

She dared to rub his arm, hoping to provide some comfort. "You are a saint."

"Nah. A minute ago, you thought I was the devil," he replied. "You know the worst part? I still have to live in their world."

"What do you mean?"

"When you cure people, they invite you everywhere."

"That's understandable. If I had a boat, you'd be on it."

He smiled, and she wished she could've known Julián Almodovar as a little boy.

"You're very sweet, Isabel. I have to be there tonight. I hate it."

"Be where?"

"I have to go be the local doctor at some bullshit cocktail event near Fajardo." He avoided her eyes. "I have to be the token local at some rich man's party."

She pulled him in, feeling his warmth even in the sun, and whispered.

"Do you need a date?"

SEVENTEEN

THE LIGHT GRAY EV pulled into the drop-off lane in front of the hotel. Isabel held her breath and said a little prayer as she watched Julián stride into the lobby. He wore a black blazer over a starched white shirt that made his skin glow. While she had to doll up for the party, Julián could've shown up in beachwear and everyone would stop and stare.

She tapped his arm as he was about to ask the clerk something.

"Buenas noches."

He turned and said nothing.

She wrung her hands, thinking this had been a terrible idea. "You said cocktail dress. Is this okay?"

"Oh. Wow." He caught his breath and bit his lip.

"It's too much, isn't it? I'll go change." She turned to leave, ears burning with shame, when she felt his touch.

"Please don't." He unleashed a devastating smile. "You, ah, wow. Hi. You... you look amazing. Hi."

"Are you sure this is okay?"

"You look far better than just 'okay.'" He shook his head and gazed, reaching for something. "You look... stunning. I had no idea."

She pushed him in jest. "What do you mean, you had no idea? I can clean up when I put my mind to it."

"You did. Ready?" He leaned in to kiss her cheek. He smelled delicious.

As soon as Julián left after lunch, she ran across the street to a little shop, which the owner adorably called a boutique. Isabel related the story in a torrent: a dashing local doctor wants to take me to a special party, and I need a memorable cocktail dress, stat. The owner understood. A few minutes later, Isabel smiled with satisfaction as she checked herself out in a dressing room full of pins and hopeful dreams.

The dress—black, short, and fabulous, with a strategically placed slit—accentuated everything that she felt good about. She did her hair up, just in case he liked her neck, and scored some pumps from the gal at the front desk.

Emboldened by the victory, she celebrated by exploring the streets of Condado. Wearing a hat, covering every inch of exposed skin, and leaving every possession other than her glasses and watch at the hotel, she walked into a muggy hell, staying on the well-trafficked areas of the beachside city. The mile-long journey was another study in contrasts. Garish tourist traps advertised their wares on physical signs, while more posh shops showed insanely expensive prices on tasteful AR overlays. Entire blocks of the city were razed to the ground, with no online documentation of ownership or plan. She lurched over bundles covered in white cloth, exhaling when she realized they were homeless people panhandling while escaping the blazing sun. An occasional ocean breeze broke the stench of smoke, urine, and cheap weed.

She ducked into a hotel after passing through security stiffer than an airport, and stared slack-jawed at an opulent wooden bar, beautiful and alien next to the hellish chaos outside. She drank an overpriced soda, checking out the assembled crowd. They seemed plucked from some movie and dropped into a set. Women, dressed to the nines in defiance of the heat, sauntered in with dates who could have been their grandfathers. Fat men in guayaberas and gold bracelets spouted at expats who escaped the onslaught through their phones or blinking at their glasses. Two foreign-looking businessmen considered the scene before creeping to a meeting room hidden behind a heavy oaken door. The opulence of the hotel was an affront to the people suffering outside. This was where people oblivious to reality mingled in plain sight. Perhaps this was also where the powerful and the rich decided the fate of the damned.

The walk back to the hotel passed in a blur. Three different people propositioned her—in broad daylight—as she weaved past human skeletons strung out on something that made them shiver in the heat. Others offered drugs and sex and something in foil packets that even her glasses could not identify. Navigating through broken pavement and garbage piles feet from swank restaurants and opulent boutiques, she realized there was no middle ground in Condado. Everything seemed to be a manufactured heaven, or genuine hell.

She hoped tonight would be closer to the former.

Julián opened the car door and held her hand, snapping her from the memory. The hem of her uncooperative dress rode up as she folded herself into the front seat. She didn't want Julián to think something bad, so she rocked her hips, attempting to pull it down as they made their way onto the freeway. When she caught him peeking as she turned to ask him a question, he blushed. So she crossed her legs with a satisfied smile and enjoyed the drive.

Night fell early in the tropics, plunging the island into gloom as they entered the highway. EVs and old cars sped by at maniacal speeds, weaving through traffic lanes bleached invisible by the sun. Isabel had no real experience being surrounded by gasoline-powered vehicles, and their noise shocked her.

The scenery passed in a patchwork of light and dark. Five years after the last major hurricane, people still struggled with access to electrical power. Feeble amber streetlights leaked onto piles of garbage and abandoned cars dumped on the highway shoulder, where small groups if people pushed carts or hauled grimy bags made of cloth repurposed from construction sites. A few miles later, a rider on a tricycle avoided potholes, carrying a mass of debris piled on a makeshift box. The man was visible only to the car's autopilot, and Isabel wondered if he'd arrive at his destination alive, or be obliterated by a distracted tourist.

She looked away, towards the sea. As if in brutal counterpoint, hotels and high-rises stood bright and garish in the evening sky. She felt like an alien visitor, observing the sharp contrasts while ensconced in the bubble of Julián's car.

"Those people walking on the road are going to get hurt."

Julián nodded. "A lot of them travel at night, when it cools down."

"Can't they take public transportation?"

"Bus authority went bankrupt years ago."

She sat back as they left the busiest stretch of Isla Verde behind. Julián's EV—sensible, basic, not ostentatious—was a comforting paradise compared to the plight of those outside.

After a while, she broke the silence. "So, who is throwing this party?"

"Rich guy from South Carolina who's been living here for about ten years."

"Investor?"

Julián shook his head. "Not unless you count the billionaire estates he's built. His investment in the island is limited to the mansions he financed for his buddies."

"Aren't they supposed to invest in bigger projects for those tax breaks? Not just build more homes for the rich?"

Julián tapped the wheel to let the autopilot drive and turned to her. "That ship sailed. A long time ago."

She looked outside, at the patchwork of despair alongside gleaming symbols of wealth, obvious even in the glow of evening. The extremes between rich and poor, the contrast of luxury amid destruction, now made sense.

The last twenty-four hours had heightened her awareness of the inequality blanketing her island. In exchange for promises to sink millions into the island, the government allowed expats to zero out their federal taxes, and paid a pittance in local taxes. No one was surprised at what happened next: despite massive personnel bloat, the government was somehow "unable" to oversee the expats to ensure they kept their end of the bargain. Instead of fixing the problem, Fortaleza removed all oversight for foreign investors escaping the tax collectors. The story caused a furor when it broke decades ago. It was now clear that most, including here, forgot about the injustice.

"They never tried to fix it, did they?"

"They didn't," he replied.

"I guess I'm not surprised why this story isn't on the news anymore."

"And you'd be right. Almost every CEO of a media outlet has either a house or a post office box in Puerto Rico."

"Didn't the IRS try to find all these deadbeats?"

Julián tilted his head back in a sad laugh. "The expats sent an army of lobbyists to Congress."

"I remember the hearings. They had all these slick charts on the fictional vast sums they contributed to the economy."

"Good thing they didn't go into the mathematics," Julián replied. "The expats pay a microscopic fraction of their income, but they proclaimed it loud enough that Congress lost interest. In the meantime, the Puerto Rican middle class now pays over half of their income in taxes. And that doesn't count the sales tax for the debt."

"How can people live like this?"

"They can't. Avoiding taxes is a lucrative industry in Puerto Rico," he replied with a smirk. "Plus, Fortaleza sued the IRS."

Isabel stared back, slack jawed. "The Puerto Rico Government spent money to defend people breaking their tax laws? They wanted these deadbeats to continue?"

He nodded.

"Julián, that makes no sense! I'm no economist, but doesn't the government need the revenue? They're still under the Junta!"

"The government might need revenue. But politicians need campaign contributions a lot more."

"Who the hell would vote for an idiot who gives away the island?" She found her voice rising. "Who in their right mind would vote for anyone who would raise taxes on the middle class so a bunch of rich expats can live for free? Don't they know they're creating two worlds on a tiny island? Who the hell would do that?"

Julián smiled and turned to her. "You'll meet some of them tonight."

EIGHTEEN

ISABEL HAD NEVER EXITED a car this low with a dress this short. She pivoted, knees together to not flash anyone, and tried to smile. She stepped out of the car, feeling like a baby giraffe, and a man closed the door behind her. The man—he must've been in his fifties—looked away to not embarrass her.

"Se ve preciosa, señorita," he said with a flat smile.

"Gracias," she whispered back. She wondered how he felt among such opulence, whether he was thankful for employment, or embarrassed to live as a prop in someone else's fantasy.

Julián offered his arm. "You ready?"

She nodded and strode towards the most amazing mansion she'd ever seen. The checkpoint of armed private security guards a few miles down the road now made sense. The entryway seemed wrought from an IM Pei fever dream, all angles, fountains, and marble. An open, bright foyer beckoned inside. Stately trees towered around them, dripping moon shadows onto the lawn. She'd never seen anything so extravagant.

Some crazy rich people in Palm Springs and the surrounding area might build similar mansions. But she was certain no one within a hundred miles of Tampa could afford to live like this. It bothered her to think that such opulence existed so close—and so far—from the poverty and violence she'd lived through during the past day.

A few steps before entering, she stopped. "Listen!" she hissed at Julián.

"What?"

She craned her neck to hear. "A coqui! I haven't heard one since I've been back."

Julián clenched his jaw and they walked inside.

She knew she was not overdressed the instant she stepped into the mansion. Every woman—all of them pale and out of place—glared at her as they entered the marble expanse. The older men leered, and the nouveau riche, dressed in expensive slacker couture, examined her and calculated their odds. She pulled Julián in tight.

"Please don't leave me," she whispered. He responded by squeezing her hand.

"Doctor J!" A woman in her sixties, with fake boobs and heaping servings of Botox, leaned into Julián for a cursory air kiss. "How good to see you!"

"Mrs. Rosenfeld. You look wonderful." He air-kissed the woman back and smiled. "This is my friend, Isabel."

The woman shrugged in manufactured delight. Her perfume overpowered something old. "Well, hello, dear. You've hit the jackpot."

She wanted to ask the woman if she feared her face popping open if she ever smiled for real.

"Hi," Isabel replied instead. "We're only—"

"Roger!" The woman ignored Isabel, turning towards a fat man with liver spots dragging a gaunt thirty-year-old. "Helloooo!"

Isabel watched her leave. She'd held the old hag's attention for exactly no time.

"Well, she was... nice. What was her problem? Brain transplant?"

"I can't speak about my patients." He winked at the secret between them.

An old man—tall, with a head full of white hair, tapping a gold-encrusted cane—walked up and offered a blue-veined hand.

"Ah, the young doctor returns," the man said with a southern drawl.

"Mister Thornberry." Julián nodded and smiled. "You look great."

"I have the best doctor," the man replied with a wink. "And who is this beauty?"

"Hello, sir. My name is Isabel."

"Augustus Thornberry." The old man's eyes twinkled in a bleary smile. "Please forgive an old man for being so improper, but you are beautiful and a sight to behold." He patted her hand and raised an eyebrow at Julián. "I will not pretend to know what you two are up to, but I pray it is no good."

Her cheeks flushed. They laughed and chatted about the southeast for a bit, and Augustus Thornberry excused himself to mingle with the guests.

"He's a delightful man. Is this his house?"

Julián nodded.

"My god. What did he do?"

"Made a ridiculous amount of money when the eastern states banned coal plants. Has a libertarian streak. Wanted to do the same thing here."

"How'd that turn out?"

"He tried to invest in aerospace and renewables and drug discovery. Got tired when the government lobbyists kept asking for too much. He ended up building a few homes for his buddies. Now he has parties and counts his money."

Waiters offered delectable hors d'oeuvres and replenished flutes of sinful champagne. The only young people besides her and Julián were slacker-looking frat boys with strung-out dates pouring fake boobs out of barely-there designer dresses.

"Crypto and nepo babies," he muttered, as if reading her thoughts. "Lots of trust-funders calling themselves entrepreneurs."

"Tax haven crowd?"

He nodded again. "They jet in and out to placate the IRS. They fly down when they run out of cocaine."

"How much of the money in this place is being invested in the island?"

He placed his thumb and forefinger almost touching in silent reply.

"And who builds these mansions?"

Julián raised his eyebrow and pursed his lips. "That's the extent of their investments."

She pulled his ear close to hers. "You mean to tell me that these assholes come here, and the only things they invest in are their own mansions?"

He raised his eyebrows in a clear *yes*.

"So the only jobs they're making are..."

He nodded again. "Tourism and service. They expect us locals to serve them."

She clenched her jaw. Whether to keep the scream or bile inside, she couldn't say.

"I have to ask you something." She was about to speak when an obese man in a white guayabera bumped into them.

"Ay bendito, perdóneme." The man looked up at Julián and sneered. "Oh, you."

"Hello, Judio."

"Señor Hermano to you," the chubby man spat. Isabel imagined that in another life, he probably kidnapped children by selling ice cream out of white panel vans. His greasy, dyed comb-over stuck to a head marked with liver spots.

"Of course," Julián replied. He did not glance at her, nor make any attempt at introduction, which she appreciated.

"And you are?" Judío examined her as if she were a piece of meat.

"She's a friend," Julián interrupted.

"Judío Hermano." He offered a fat hand. Isabel returned the courtesy on instinct and immediately regretted the gesture.

In a flash, she remembered. The man before her had presided over the dirtiest group of politicians the island had ever seen. She remembered the tale: horrific jokes on a long-defunct social media app, making fun of the old, the dying, the damned, all while boasting about their political influence, posting photos from parties with Hollywood gliteratti too stupid to do background checks. The depravity of that group—of this man—had so infected the halls of Fortaleza that the governor was forced to resign in an historic, embarrassing moment.

This monster had single-handedly set back the island decades. People around the world still spoke of La Fortaleza as a cesspool of corruption, twenty-five years after the storm which ushered them in. And here he was, surviving political Armageddon like a cockroach, still mingling with the rich, thankful for the crumbs they gave him, too stupid to understand they were charity for a loser and nothing more.

She wanted to confront the man, to ask him how he still dared to live here, when another man approached Judío with a hug.

"Judío! ¡Coño, te estás poniendo viejo!"

"Estoy como coco," Judío replied. Isabel had never been this happy to be ignored in her life. "Como estás, Elodio?"

Cold washed over her. People spoke of Elodio Santos only in whispers. Santos had been the power behind the throne of so many Puerto Rican Governors, that people had lost count. She'd seen pictures of him as a young man: handsome, with cruel eyes that radiated a disturbing self-awareness. Elodio must've been pushing eighty, but looked fit and hungry.

He nodded a vague greeting at Julián, then undressed Isabel with a glance. He bowed, staring through his eyebrows, and flashed the perfect teeth of a predator's smile.

"Buenas noches, señorita. Who do I have the pleasure to meet?"

"My name is Isabel," she said. She tried to not touch him, but his stare defied her.

He made a big deal of kissing her hand. She'd disinfect her entire arm after that.

"You are not from here," he declared.

"Raised in Tampa." She glanced at Julián, who looked terrified.

"Oh!" Santos changed in an instant. "Are you visiting or relocating to our beautiful island?"

She was about to say "none of your damn business" but caught herself.

"My father left a trust. I'm thinking of moving." She summoned every ounce of high school drama club to wink and not spit at him. "They say the best way to make money is to avoid giving it away."

"Wise words, young lady. Would you be relocating as an investor?"

Isabel nodded. "Is there any other way?"

"Wise beyond her years, this one." Santos grinned and raised an eyebrow at Julián. "Well, if you need anything, here's my card."

He handed over a small, square piece of white cardboard with his name and number. It took her a moment to figure out what he meant.

She held the card with both hands, the way she'd read in an old Japanese book. "Thanks. I'll keep you in mind."

Santos tipped his head. "I'm sorry?"

"Just that I still haven't decided. How to proceed, you know?"

He flashed a pained smile full of disdain. "It can be difficult to get things done in our beautiful island. Unless you know the right people. Those willing to help."

Then he left, holding Judío's arm, headed into the crowd of people.

"I'd like to leave."

She thought she'd be the one to say that first, but Julián beat her to it. He sounded terrified.

NINETEEN

"I HAVEN'T SEEN one of these in ten years," Isabel said as she examined Elodio's business card. "Doesn't he have a wallet on his phone, or his watch?"

Julián had been quiet since entering the car. Once past the security guards—who asked why they were leaving so early—he finally relaxed.

"Elodio didn't trust you," he murmured.

"Trust me? What do you mean?"

"You didn't immediately thank him for his offer to help."

"What was I supposed to do? Thank him for being a lecherous scumbag?"

"Maybe he was hedging. Didn't recognize you and thought you were undercover."

"Do I look like I'm undercover?" She gestured at her dress, riding way too high for her comfort. She rocked her hips to pull the hem down. "I'd have nowhere to hide a gun."

He flashed a thin smile. "I'm sorry we had to leave so early. You look wonderful tonight."

"You are very sweet. What happened back there?"

He waited to respond until they turned onto a wide highway headed west. To their right, the lights of cargo ships twinkled over the water. Ahead, a tunnel of light and chaos, alien from the luxury they'd escaped. The car extended that world, a capsule moving through the island, forgoing contact or interaction. She imagined the expats insisted on taking the bubble with them, to remain in the rarefied air that traveled from one lavish hideout to the next.

"Did you recognize them?"

She nodded. "Judío was the scumbag who injected himself into everything and embarrassed that governor with the social media disaster." She gazed at the garbage and debris piled by the road. "The other guy—"

He raised a hand, then put a finger to his lips. "Can I see your phone?"

"I don't use a phone, Julián." She gestured her watch at him.

"Can I have it?"

She rolled her eyes and unclasped the band. He pressed a button on the center console, opening a hidden cavity. He dropped his handset and her watch and closed it.

Then he tapped the autopilot, pressed his finger on a digital pad under the power button, and the car went dark.

"Julián! What the—"

"Car's still driving. You're safe, and we're fine. No one can hear us."

The steering wheel followed the road as the car continued the route home.

"What the heck is going on?" Her skin froze in alarm. "Oh, my god. You're undercover!"

He chuckled, which made her feel better. "I wish. No. Our friend Roberto taught me a few tricks, and I bought a few toys."

"Why the secrecy?"

"Because of the clinic. Fede and I mostly talk while driving. Don't want anyone to hear."

"You guys are paranoid."

He shook his head. "Maybe not enough. Elodio Santos gave you a card. He'll be expecting you."

"He's just a geriatric asshole trying to impress a young girl. I can take care of myself. I don't need his help."

"He expects you to need his help."

"I don't want to deal with someone like that."

"I don't think you understand." He shut his eyes tight. "No one says 'no' to him. Why do you think nothing has ever happened to him?"

She furrowed her brow in thought. Julián was right: after decades of loud whispers about blatant corruption, some people remained inexplicably unbothered.

"Color me curious. Why?"

"That man," he pointed his thumb behind him, "has been the gatekeeper for every administration on this island for decades. Everyone knows, and no one has ever caught him. Not even now. Why?"

"Same reason the Mafia is hard to track?" She shrugged. "They're professional."

"Keep going. What do you mean?"

"They cover all the bases. Plan for every eventuality. He's—"

Her hair stood on end.

"Say it. Say what's on your mind."

"Elodio... has the Feds on his payroll?"

Julián nodded. "Not everyone. Only a handful. Go on."

"DC?"

He nodded again. "Makes generous contributions to ensure nothing gets done. Easiest job for certain members of Congress."

There it was: the reason for her island being stuck in the twentieth century—or before—while the rest of the world moved forward. Outside, a light mist pocked the windshield. After a few seconds, the wipers cleared them off.

"Do you know there are people in Washington who want Puerto Rico to fail?"

"That sounds like a conspiracy theory, Julián."

"Maybe not fail, but they don't want it to change. Which is the same thing." He blew out his cheeks and continued. "One representative, in Congress for decades, received millions in campaign contributions from a PAC that fought against Federal oversight of funds. Can you imagine it? A member of Congress taking actions to not protect taxpayers from graft?"

"I don't believe that."

"Fair enough. I'll send you the link. Another relocated to the island after twenty-plus years in Washington and somehow bought a mansion in his hometown. On a Congressional salary, of course. Guess what under what party he ran for governor?"

Isabel shook her head.

"Three different separatist parties. Let that sink in. This man swore to uphold the Constitution, but behind the scenes, he was lobbying for Puerto Rico to remain 'separate but unequal,' so he could have a run at his second political career."

She nodded at the recollection. "My mom told me about him. I thought the stories were more manufactured news. No one could be that despicable. Everyone assumed it was all a joke."

"It wasn't. How about the millions lobbyists send to the middle east, just to keep the island on bunker?"

"I don't understand."

"How do you get your power in Tampa?"

"Every house has solar. The state is divesting from single-use solar farms and focusing on renewables in a big way. Renewable energy is the second fastest industry in Florida."

He nodded. "For a few years, it was the same here. Residential solar was booming. Then someone decided they couldn't make money from sunlight. And the Oversight Board suddenly realized they couldn't pay off the debt if people had the power to make their own choices. That's when the owners of that natural gas project convinced the governor to tax solar. For several administrations, every Federal secretary of energy came down to see how Puerto Rico was recovering from Hurricane Maria. No one bothered to ask why we still shipped millions of gas into San Juan. A few years later, they went back to importing bunker oil. Stuff so dirty, no one uses in the third world."

She turned in her seat to face him. "That's impossible. They don't even do that in the Middle East."

"You are correct. Many people have made a fortune ensuring Puerto Rico never moves forward."

TWENTY

THE WORDS STUNNED HER.

"Julián, that's ridiculous. That would be treason."

"Who do you think goes to those events? Everyone parties with this veneer of selflessness, of coming to our island to save us from ourselves. One bribe later, most realize all they have to do is grease the palms of people like Elodio and never work again."

"You are telling me elected officials in DC and San Juan want Puerto Rico to fail?"

He nodded again.

"I'm sorry, but that makes no sense." She crossed her arms in a huff. "Some of those guys were huge statehood supporters back in the day. Don't they want our island to improve so they can join the US?"

Julián laughed out loud. "The greatest trick the political class ever played was creating the illusion that status was everything."

"Okay, color me curious. Go on?"

"In Puerto Rico, the question of status is a religion." The fury in his eyes reflected the lights outside. "And when your opponent is of a different religion, you'll forgive any sin."

She remembered it well. The only constant from her island—since the day of her birth—had been an unending parade of political crises that boggled the mind. In any other country, such malfeasance would've caused massive change. Here it became yesterday's news as quickly as the weather.

"Every governor since Hurricane Maria has been involved in a major scandal. And people still vote for them. Why?" He shook his head. "Our voters are no longer choosing anything. They've been conditioned to make sure the other guy doesn't get in."

"C'mon Julián." She turned away, resting her elbow on the car door. "Don't people take civics in grade school?"

"Have you seen the schools here? They're the worst in the nation. It's an embarrassment." He shook his head in exasperation. "Let's just say that our local political class wouldn't appreciate an educated voter. All they want is to perpetuate the myth of status. When something irrelevant becomes the most important thing, it becomes religion: the source of every sin and the forgiveness of every transgression." He paused for a moment and flashed an angry smile. "Except this religion is a hoax. It doesn't exist."

"What do you mean?"

"How many plebiscites and votes has Puerto Rico held on status?"

Since her phone was in some digital vault inches from her, she counted on her fingers instead. At four, Julián interrupted.

"It doesn't matter. None of them mean anything. They are all political kabuki theater to keep two and a half million Puerto Ricans focused on something else."

She wanted to argue, but knew better. She'd seen that brand of political religiosity brought to the mainland by those about to enter the Puerto Rican diaspora. Months after they left the island, the century-long debate on status no longer mattered.

"It is like nothing has changed in fifty years."

"Nothing has," he replied. "Except we're poorer, sicker, and dying. In another generation, if we do nothing, the island will be a bunch of rich enclaves surrounded by a welfare state. Anyone who works for a living will have long gone to the mainland." He shook his head yet again. "I can't look away while that happens."

"Santos is the gatekeeper." Her heart pounded her throat. "There's no room for anyone to upset the status quo. Because if they do, the machinery crumbles. And the powerful will never let that happen."

He whispered a quiet "yes," and they sat in silence for miles.

After a while, he placed a finger on his lips, then pointed at the console. He pulled her watch from the cavity, and after a few taps, the inside of the car blinked to life.

"Huh. Just in time." He pointed at the center screen. A large swath of red, with several pulsing dots, lay a few miles ahead.

"What is it?"

"If I were to bet, a gang shootout on Baldorioty Avenue." He tapped the screen and a blue route threaded around the carnage. "We'll be fine."

They pulled off on the highway exit before the airport. The gleaming high-rises of Isla Verde towered over the coast, out of place in the disorder. They meandered on Isla Verde Avenue, in light traffic crawling among some of the nicest vehicles Isabel had ever seen. After the last hotel, the road twisted away from the coast before retaking the path toward Condado.

The change in the pavement announced the demarcation. Potholes, deep as beach balls, pocked the asphalt, and structures dating from the 1960s—covered in weeds peeking behind iron grates and barbed wire—stood in the gloom of intermittent light. Several ocean-side lots glinted in the dark, submerged under the encroaching sea.

After another mile, they arrived at the outskirts of Condado. This stretch of road was dry. A concrete wall protected trendy buildings from the receding coast and blocked the view of the ocean.

In less than two miles, they had driven past luxuriant opulence, through desolation, and back to riches. The poor remained powerless against the onslaught of nature. The rich used the sweat of the locals to defy it.

She clung to the awareness that she was still attuned to the chasm between worlds. It was too easy to travel from pocket to pocket, never setting foot on where the true Puerto Ricans lived. Driving in a nice car was like traveling by spaceship: the comfort of a cocoon that carried your world from one point to the next.

Julián stopped at the passenger drop-off at the hotel.

"One more night here?"

"I guess." Isabel shrugged. "I'll stay here as long as your friend will have me." She gazed at him and smiled. "If that is okay with you."

"You're welcome for as long as she needs you. I'll walk you in."

She unlocked the lobby door with her watch. It was late, but the attendant was still on duty, like at an old-time hotel. She did notice two burly armed guards patrolling the lobby, just in case.

Julián walked her to the elevator. She wanted to tell him it was okay, that she could go up on her own, but said nothing. They stared into space as the elevator sped up to her floor and walked in silence to her door.

"Thank you for a lovely evening." Her heart raced.

"Thanks for asking me if I needed a date," he replied. "Isabel, I—"

Her heart stopped. "What?"

"I'm sorry I unloaded all that on you. I get very frustrated whenever I have to meet those people." He took a deep breath, and tried to smile. "But it's not all bad. There are good people here still. Everywhere. I'm sorry if I was a downer tonight."

She reached for his hand. "Please don't apologize. I cannot tell you how much I appreciate your honesty."

"You are amazing, Isabel. Thank you for going with me. Good night."

He leaned in for a social kiss, the innocent peck on the cheek to say "'goodnight". She stopped him, fell into his eyes, then melter her lips on his.

"Buy me a coffee tomorrow?"

He nodded in shock. She kissed him again, swept into her room, and closed the door with a smile.

TWENTY-ONE

THIS TIME, she woke up much earlier.

Isabel opened the balcony window, coughing from the fumes in the steamy morning. Rock doves cooed the sun into the sky, and the aroma of sweet bread and coffee parted the stench of garbage, lifting her spirits. Ten floors high, the noise of morning traffic, gunshots, and gasoline generators wafted away. The sprawl of San Juan extended south, crawling from the dawn slumber.

Despite the ever-present tang of garbage suspended in the breeze, the island felt clean and calm this early, full of possibility. Perhaps, she thought, that explained the several pairs of runners ambling up and down the patched and cracked sidewalks of Condado Avenue. Everyone tried to escape the heat. No one escaped the humidity, the smoke, or the decay.

She did a little yoga, some core exercises, and a few squats before showering. After trying on three outfits, she settled on a little sundress and sandals. Her heart raced as she did her hair and picked out the right lip gloss. She considered not wearing her glasses, wanting no distractions to intrude her time with Julián.

Protecting her eyes from the relentless sun won out, so she blinked the sequence to mute her notifications.

The twenty minutes waiting by the door dragged on forever. When her watch beeped she descended into the lobby, sauntered out of the elevator into the steamy morning, and entered the bakery next door.

Julián stood up from a table in the corner. She said a little silent prayer, hoping the kiss had not made it awkward between them, and smiled through her nerves.

"Hi," he whispered.

"Hi," she replied.

They stood still, unsure of where to start after last night. After forever, she played it safe, and leaned in for the harmless and friendly peck on the cheek, the custom even among acquaintances. When their cheeks touched, he turned, gentle and soft, and nuzzled his lips on her skin. A delicious shiver raced through her. He smelled like day at the beach.

"I got you a cortado and a quesito." He gestured at the seat next to him. "I hope you don't mind."

She bit her lip to not burst into giggles. "Thank you." The cortado was perfect, the quesito was perfect, and the day promised everything.

"I really enjoyed last night. Thanks for taking me."

He said nothing for a while. "Thanks for coming. And for allowing me to show you. I didn't know how much I needed to let all that out."

"I'm glad I could be there." She squeezed his hand. "How was your night?"

"Short drive. I live in Santurce."

"Minutes away, then. How long have you been there?"

"I bought into one of those new apartment developments. One of the few that worked as expected. I was lucky."

The confusion on her face must've been obvious.

"Remember our chat about the expat investors?" He glanced around him, seeking privacy. "Some of them had ethics. They tried to honor the intent of the tax haven by bringing in business and hiring people. But they were the tiny minority." He took a thoughtful sip of his coffee. "Most of them believe that building expensive mansions for their fellow tax cheats somehow qualifies as 'investment.' The apartment complex I live in is one of the few exceptions that worked."

"Why does this happen, Julián? Don't the politicians know this?"

"They do, Isabel. But they ignore it. The incentives have been wrong for a century."

"'Be careful what you incentivize, because you just might get it.' That was my economics professor at UF."

"I like that. Do you know how much the Governor of Puerto Rico makes?"

"I have no idea. Close to seven figures? I'm assuming he'd be the lowest-paid state executive in the US."

"Good guess. He gets paid $70,000."

She had to cover her mouth to not spit out her coffee. "What? That is close to poverty level in most of the US!"

"Yep. Hasn't changed since 2012, I believe."

"That's almost forty years ago! And it wasn't a lot of money then!"

"Exactly. But if the head of the government, by law, can't even buy food on his salary, imagine how cheap it would be for someone to change his mind."

The words took the air out of her chest. "Julián, you're saying graft is baked into Puerto Rican politics."

He nodded with a sad smile. "Legislature passed the law before you or I were born. Their pay is higher, by the way. They justified it by saying the Governor lives in Fortaleza, blah blah. You can figure out where that is going."

"And I can already imagine who benefits from it."

He tilted his head and leaned close. "You met some of them last night."

Her hands quivered as she sipped her coffee. Julián wasn't lying, complaining, or chasing conspiracies. Everything he'd told her over the past two nights she'd never forget—were confirmed by experience. The executive director for her nonprofit had been right: Isabel needed to see this firsthand.

So why was no one talking about this? Why was the island still consumed with gossip, music, and made-up scandals when the very fabric of the government was purpose-built to keep the unelected in power?

"Julián, I know so much is wrong, but..." She looked away, searching for words. "That place last night was sumptuous. If something like that exists here, doesn't it say something? That maybe at least a little part of our island works?"

He said nothing for a moment, then took a deep breath.

"Want to go for a ride?"

TWENTY-TWO

THEY WEAVED their way out of Condado, onto a short stretch of Baldorioty Avenue, then through the Minillas Tunnel before entering the freeway west. Julián's car zipped along, quiet and steady, vibrating over the worst pavement Isabel had ever felt in her life.

The outskirts of Condado and Miramar were a study in contrasts. Modern apartment buildings loomed over streets so destroyed by weather that cars had to avoid potholes capable of swallowing a typical sedan. Cute restaurants and shops stood side-by-side with homes that appeared blown out or burned, many bearing graffiti, which Julián informed her were signs for junkies and drops. Vegetation grew everywhere, clutching in desperation to the concrete that covered the island.

The smell overcame everything. When the wind was just right, the stench from overfilled landfills far past capacity crawled in her nose like a sickness. Trying to breathe through her mouth made it worse. The acrid smog of dirty oil and diesel and gasoline irritated her eyes and burned her lungs. Only near the water, where the rich had staked their claim, could the ocean air wash away the putrid decay.

They headed west in their air-conditioned bubble, passing antiquated billboards that provided a spark of humor to the desolation. The signs for gas stations were numerous and shocking. On the sweeping curve leaving Guaynabo and the prison to Bayamón, she saw several cars abandoned on the road—blackened and vandalized —and wondered what had forced the occupants to flee.

"Where are we going? Dorado?"

"We'll start there."

Isabel fought a pang of guilt as they passed the exit to Bayamón. Titi Luisa recovered in some ward she'd never be able to find, while Isabel sped west, clad in a cute sundress with a gorgeous physician toward a day of adventure. The anticipation of what she'd discover lodged in her throat.

"She's fine." Julián nodded in her direction, as if reading her thoughts. "Fede called me this morning. They're keeping her sedated until she heals. She's sleeping, but stable."

She squeezed his hand and did not want to let go.

The sky broke into a brilliant blue. The emerald hills to their left reached into the heavens, taking her breath away. Puerto Rico —her home—was beautiful.

He squeezed her hand back. "What's on your mind?"

"I was just thinking about how pretty our island is," Isabel replied. "Few people see this."

"The inside secret is that our beaches are pretty terrible. But our food and the mountains more than make up for it."

"Will you take me there? The mountains?"

He tapped the autopilot on the car and turned toward her.

"I'm sorry." Her cheeks flushed in embarrassment before he could answer. "I know you're probably busy and—"

"No. There is nothing I'd want to do more." His eyes drilled into her soul. Then he flashed a little smile, innocent and genuine, and turned back to the road. "But first, I want to show you a few things."

After a few minutes, they took the exit to Dorado. "Prepare yourself," he said as they slowed down.

Had the car been a spaceship that whisked her away from Tampa, she would have never known she left. Dorado—it amazed her they still called it by a Spanish name—reminded her of the exurbs of Tampa. The fabric of the place—strip malls instead of cozy thoroughfares, clear-cut parking areas instead of twisty streets —differed from every other place she'd seen. Dorado was to Puerto Rico what Los Angeles might have been to Saint Augustine. The sterile familiarity transplanted from an ocean away was a sickening affront.

"We won't stop here. I don't think you'll mind."

She did not, staring slack-jawed at the imported desolation around them. "There are no homes on the streets anymore," Julián said, gesturing at tidy and artificial storefronts. "Mainland developers bought and developed every home in sight. It's like a Potemkin village. They razed the town so they could replace it."

"Looks clean, at least." "All the new construction pushed the locals out. They live a few miles away from here."

"It's like they invaded the place," she muttered. They drove past remodeled storefronts, which now bore foreign names in chic holo signs. The main strip reminded her of those manufactured Vegas "main streets" so popular back in the 2020s.

"Did you see a beach?"

"No. I thought we were pretty far away."

He shook his head. "We were very close to the coast. All beaches in Puerto Rico are supposed to be public. Except here."

"Did they change the law?"

"You don't have to change the law. You just have to pay off people so they don't enforce it." He smiled, sad and angry. "The government allowed the expats to build breakers, so the locals—like you and me—can't infiltrate their beaches."

Her stomach soured. They drove through a strip that belonged in Boca, or Brandon, or some other cookie-cutter hellscape. Everything was so clean and neat it appeared artificial. Barely a mile beyond the edge of downtown, the imported architecture fell away as tall grasses and gnarled trees took control of the side of the roads.

"Let me show you where the locals in Dorado live now."

Julián turned left into a small neighborhood only a few streets in size. The homes—all chipped concrete and barred windows—seemed blasted by the sun. Abandoned vehicles, furniture, and garbage dominated the dry lawns and the cracking pavement. Some homes dripped with faded blue tarps Isabel knew dated from the aftermath of Cat 6 hurricanes a decade past. The only living thing was a skinny cat panting in the shade of a red-tiled balcony covered in rusting iron grates.

"Julián, this is..."

"Abject poverty. Fifteen years ago, the mayor boasted about how many expats were moving to Dorado, telling everyone how much in taxes they contributed to the economy. Guess where the taxes went?"

"Please don't say what I think you're going to say."

"Yep. His pockets. The town tried to vote him out. His opponent somehow dropped his candidacy and bought a mansion in Hialeah."

She was quiet as Julián weaved his way past piles of garbage spilling onto the street.

"I can imagine where they all work now. Services and tourism for the tax haven crowd?"

He clenched his jaw. "You'd be right."

Gentrification, injustice, and displacement had dominated her visit. She wondered how much more of her birthplace had been stolen, how many more had been forced from their homes so wealthy tax-haven patrons could avoid "the locals" and continue their unencumbered, magical lives.

They left the neighborhood behind and returned to the freeway, heading west. After a few kilometers—the island still used the metric system for distance, an artifact of Spanish rule—the scenery changed. Karst hills dotted the landscape to the south, and beyond, the lush emerald green of the mountains blended into clouds that turned to sky. They pulled off a several exits west of Dorado.

This part of the island was in another world. Hunched figures sheltered themselves from the heat with cardboard and cloth. Zoning had been forgotten long ago given the mishmash of barred stores, abandoned cars, and fruit stands dotting the unending cracked concrete. Feral animals—she hoped they were cats—weaved through the garbage and weeds, hiding from the glare. The fading, scrawled signs advertising mangoes or avocados for sale were the only proof she was not in some lost corner of the world.

"Is it all like this?"

"A lot of it is," he replied.

They entered what appeared to be the outskirts of a neighborhood. Every home sported more of the thick, rusted bars over every opening, consigning the inhabitants to personal jails. Abandoned, disgorged cars dotted the shoulder and sidewalks. No walkers complained about the obstacles. Julián's dash indicated the temperature reached one hundred and five degrees. Much hotter, and a human would cook in this humidity. No shade remained. Imposing, graffitied stumps marked where majestic trees once stood.

Less than a mile later, they pulled into an open-air restaurant. Wooden chairs and tiled tables sat under a thick concrete overhang. Metal fans attached to misters kept the shaded area somewhat tolerable in the thick heat that blasted everything.

The restaurant seemed stuck in the beginning of the century. Sticky, laminated menus offered dishes with scratched-off prices. She examined the images as Julián ordered mojitos at the bar.

Her jaw dropped when he set them on the table.

"Something wrong?"

"Those are plastic cups!"

"Yeah. Glass is expensive and easy to steal."

She examined the cup as if it was poisonous. "You can't recycle plastic. You have to throw it away." She stared at Julián as if he didn't understand. "And we live on an island."

He smiled as if he knew where she was going and took a sip of his drink.

"Don't tell me." She took a long drag of her mojito, feeling guilty until she savored the sweet snap of lime, mint, and rum. "The government makes money off the landfills. Even if they're overfilled."

"You are learning more about Puerto Rico every minute."

She raised her arms in defeat. "Is there anything here that works? Anyplace where political graft doesn't make the island worse?"

He held up the drink in appreciation. "We make our own rum. And we don't import lime or mint." He winked with a big smile. "But we import the sugar from Cuba."

She tilted her head in acknowledgement, and they toasted to the world.

Most of the food was familiar: chillo, masitas, mofongo, and alcapurrias. Some items she'd never seen.

"What's 'de palo' mean? It's pretty cheap compared to everything else."

Julián shook his head and pointed to a lone tree outside. "Don't order those. Iguana meat."

She spit out a mint leaf. "What?"

"They took over a lot of our ecosystems over the past twenty years. Only way to control them is to eat them."

"Julián, that is gross."

"Half the price of chicken. That is how much of the island now gets their protein."

"What about fish?"

"Scan the prices."

She scanned the QR codes on the sticky plastic menu. "My god," she whispered. "How can people afford this?"

"The locals don't," he replied. "Places like this live off tourism, or the few expats who want to 'connect' with the locals."

Julián ordered some *chillo a la plancha with tostones*, and Isabel had *mofongo de yuca* with *carne frita*. The order felt excessive, but Julián explained that their meal would make the restaurant profitable for the week. Every waiter, cook, and dishwasher would have a paycheck, which meant food, energy, and hope.

Their food arrived with a minimum of fuss. It was everything she could've hoped for, a connection to home and joy and comfort. Everything tasted better in the open air. The breeze—hot, laden with salt and sea—blasted away the decay and disappointment, caressing her skin at a rhythm that made her feel at peace. All the injustice, iniquity, and depredation wafted away, pushed into oblivion by a pearlescent string of perfect moments that knit a memorable afternoon—and for some, a life.

Perhaps, she realized, this was it: when you lived in paradise, the pleasures of the garden took your attention away from the snakes.

TWENTY-THREE

THEY DROVE WEST, weaving in and out of the rugged karst hills that hid towns deeper inland. Ancient trees framed the highway, open some stretches, intimate and inviting the next. Flamboyanes and palms stood apart from avocado and mango trees, and many more she could not name. They swept onto the seaside a handful of miles after turning north.

Isabel recognized the road—"la número dos," one of three loop roads built a century ago by the Army Corps of Engineers, once encircling the island when it was the epicenter of the Cold War.

"My mother's family was from here," she murmured.

"Arecibo?"

She nodded. "I don't think I've ever been there."

He nodded, eyes far up the road.

Signs of progress turned intermittent the further they traveled from the highway. The artificial neatness of imported order chipped away, replaced by what Isabel now knew to be the real island, stuck at the beginning of the century. Without the ubiquitous gas stations, the small towns of Hatillo and Camuy could've been plucked from a documentary holo about the south of Spain.

They entered Quebradillas, old and sparse, on a pockmarked highway that split communities in two. Coffee shops, bakeries, and nail salons emerged from piles of rubbish and tires scattered along the road. They continued on as the road hugged green cliffs overlooking the sea and pulled off into an expansive overlook.

Someone had vandalized the tourist center's restrooms and information board, abandoned years ago. Concrete ledges, chipped and covered in fading graffiti, crumbled under the onslaught of salt, sea, and sun.

She looked out towards the coast and caught her breath.

"I've seen this before."

An emerald promontory jutted into the Atlantic, with a thin strip of rock shielding a stone path leading to a tunnel through the bluff.

"This is Guajataca," she said into the wind. "I've seen images of this since I was a little girl."

"What do you remember?"

She held her hat against the salt breeze. The Atlantic, angry and hot, crashed against dark rocks, almost engulfing the tunnel. The small spit of land seemed to challenge the waves. "It was all dirty and covered in graffiti and garbage. Did they clean it after Hurricane Maria? It looks beautiful."

"They sold it."

She almost lost the grip on her hat. "What?"

"It belongs to a developer now. They were going to build mansions on top of the rock." He pointed at the green scrub atop the promontory. "A group of locals took it to court. It's now on hold at UNESCO. In the meantime, now you have to pay a fee to go through."

"Julián, this belongs to the island! To us!"

He shrugged in agreement. "Neither the city nor Fortaleza had money for upkeep. Last time I was here as a kid, it was a mess. Garbage all over the place, shit and urine and beer cans everywhere.

Some rich tax haven guy said he'd fix it. Probably greased the skids with a hefty political donation. He must've forgotten to tell the government he was going to turn it into mansions for his crypto buddies."

"Don't they have zoning laws? You can't build a home on protected sites like this!"

Julián laughed into the breeze. "Zoning is only for the poor. The government will gladly sell the entire island for money."

She stared at him, at the beauty torn from them, at the sea. This was not the fate her home deserved.

She snapped an image with her glasses and whispered a query. "Tell me who owns that property."

The search took no time.

The historic Guajataca Railway Tunnel straddles the municipalities of Isabela and Quebradillas in Puerto Rico. It provides passage to the former Playa el Pelícano, closed since 2035. The land over the tunnel was sold to a private buyer in 2037. No additional information is available.

"Do people know? That the expats are buying our land bit by bit and no one can even find out who they are?"

He nodded.

"Why doesn't anyone do anything about it?"

"Bread and circus. Baile, botella y baraja. It's easy to boil the frog when the water's perfect."

They turned their backs to the ocean, walked back to Julián's car, and drove on. Several miles later, after turning inland from cliffs overlooking the raging Atlantic, Julián slowed the car at a hidden left turn.

"That way is more of what we've seen." He pointed west, following the road leading west before gesturing to the narrow road. "This way you'll get to see reality."

She nodded, and the EV accelerated onto a country lane pulled straight from documentaries about the last century. Ancient trees blocked out most of the hazy sky, invading sidewalks long abandoned to the island's unrelenting green. Small homes, set well back from the pavement, stood squat and bright in the heat. The scrubby crabgrass that survived the sandy karst dominated their lawns. Concrete houses sported metal grates covering every entrance, as if the inhabitants lived in jails of their own creation.

Anywhere else, the pastel riot would've passed as quaint and inviting, but Isabel wondered if the chosen shade was the cheapest available. Dilapidated wood poles held up decrepit transformers and frayed electrical lines. She realized with a start that she had not seen above-ground power lines in Dorado. Whoever built that city hardened the grid against storms. These families lived in a different world. None of the homes on this stretch of road would be used as images to sell paradise to dilettante tourists.

They pulled into a long driveway a few meters past a lot with a SOLD sign over a fading "*Se Vende*" sign. Chickens in various states of surprise fluttered as the silent vehicle approached. They stepped out into the heat, into the pungency of farm life, the air heavy with humidity and smoke. The far-off murmur of generators drummed into her skin.

Julián stepped into the shade of the concrete patio and knocked on a screen door behind an iron grate covered in chipped white paint.

"Sí?"

"Doña Sara, es Julián."

A short woman who reminded Isabel of a walnut opened the screen door and smiled. "Ay, doctor. ¡Que alegría! Come in."

"I brought a friend. I hope you don't mind."

The woman beamed at Isabel with rheumy, wet eyes. "Que Dios te bendiga, bella. Entren, por favor."

They entered a low living room, sparse of furniture, smelling of dry leaves and cooking oil. A film of dust and smog covered the polished tile floor.

"¡Siéntense, por favor!" Doña Sara scurried to pull chairs around a small sofa. "Bienvenidos a su casa. ¿Un café?"

"Thank you, we're only passing by. I wanted to check in on you."

Isabel was about to ask when Doña Sara lit up with a smile. "This is the best doctor in Puerto Rico," she whispered. "I would not be here if it wasn't for him."

"Doña Sara," Julián added, "Is Federico's great aunt."

"Dios mío. I just met him."

"Oh, my." She leaned over and held Isabel's hand. "Was somebody sick?"

"My aunt. She... had a stroke. Federico was—"

"Ay bendito." She squeezed Isabel's hands. "No te preocupes. She's going to be fine. Look at me!"

She tried to control her emotions but failed. Doña Sara reminded her too much of Luisa, recovering alone at a clinic that did not exist, in a birthplace reeking of injustice. She fought back tears and felt Doña Sara rubbing her back.

"Everything is going to be alright. Con la ayuda de Dios."

After a few moments, the woman stood and brought back a filter pitcher and heavy, opaque glasses. "I am sorry I don't have much. But I do have ice if you need any?"

"We're fine," Isabel replied as she wiped her eyes. Condensation puddled on the table's sticky varnish. "This is perfect."

Julián took a long sip. "How is everything?"

The old woman shrugged her shoulders in apparent defeat. "We're back to the diet of the old days. Rice and beans, when we can find them."

"At least it's healthy, right?"

"¡Más vale!" she replied with a chuckle. "We have enough eggs and chickens, as long as the snakes don't eat them."

Isabel straightened in her chair and glanced around her. "Snakes?"

"Puerto Rico now has a problem with iguanas and constrictors," Julián explained. "Good thing people didn't bring rattlesnakes as pets."

"Florida was full of pythons for a decade," she added. "At least the coquis survived."

Julián and Doña Sara exchanged a sad look.

"I heard them last night. At that..." She stopped, mouth agape. An ancient sadness took her. "That was a recording?"Julián nodded."They're gone?"

"It has been a decade. They survived climate change and pandemics and diesel smoke. Exotic pets finally did them in."

"The nights are sad and quiet," Doña Sara added.

Her ears rang as she sat back, remembering. As a young girl, terrified of her new home, Isabel struggled to sleep. One magical night, her mother sat with her and played a soft sound on her phone: ko-KEE... ko-KEE...

For years, she could only fall asleep to the recorded sounds of the tiny frogs that serenaded Puerto Rican nights. Their image was the one symbol, more powerful than any other, that united the diaspora. Centuries of Puerto Rican children had been lulled into slumber by the soft, comforting sound of the coquí, the one treasure belonging to everyone, the song that rang in everyone's mind and flowed in their shared blood.

No longer. Nights in this new Puerto Rico were not held spellbound by the songs of nature she still played to lull herself to sleep. The noise of the generators people needed to stay alive now ripped the dark. The thought of belching smoke and the ever-present roar sickened her.

She took a sip of water to fight back the loss. The coquí was gone, replaced by—what? For the first time she noticed the dull silence. The din of portable generators had not infected Doña Sara's little house.

"You don't have a generator, Doña Sara. How do you have electricity?"

The old woman clapped her hands in delight. "Federico bought me panels, so we had to go off-grid to not pay '*la deuda*.' I have a battery that keeps me going. And a little propane generator out back in case there's a hurricane."

"Why don't more people do that?" Isabel asked. "Solar and batteries are cheap."

"Not here," Julián added. "The Junta and the power company didn't like it when people went with solar."

"The entire world is powered by renewables now, Julián. Our government can't ignore science and the future."

"But they do need to pay off a debt. If everyone goes solar, they can't pay it back. Guess who got stuck with the bill?"

"Are you telling me that rich guy yesterday can have solar, but if Doña Sara does the same, she's penalized?"

He nodded.

"And I imagine he's not paying extra taxes to pay back the debt, right?"

"I think their lawyers would say 'my client relocated to the island post-bankruptcy and thus should not be liable for prior government obligations.' I've heard that a hundred times."

She swallowed back bile. "I'm so sorry, Doña Sara. This is so unfair."

"Don't worry, nena. The politicians have been doing that for a hundred years."

They tried to laugh, and sipped water as dust motes floated in the thick, still air.

"We should go. Thanks for having us. I'm so happy you're doing so well." Julián stood up and tapped something on his watch. Doña Sara turned to her buzzing phone and frowned in delight.

"Ay bendito, no..."

"Please take it," Julián said with a smile.

Doña Sara stood up and hugged him, murmuring "Que Dios te bendiga," and making the sign of the cross on his chest with her tiny, gnarled hands.

She held on to Julián as they stepped outside. "How's Roberto?"

He stared at the dirt. "He's better."

"Tell him I send him *la bendición*. Remember, you have each other."

"I will," he replied, and they crawled off through the dirt driveway with a wave. Back on the main road, they headed west toward Aguadilla.

"She's a special lady. That's very noble that you take such good care of her."

"I've known her since I was a little boy. Patched up my scrapes many times. Maybe that's why I went into medicine."

"How does she know Roberto?"

He was quiet for a while. "Did he tell you about his sister?"

She nodded. "Told me she died visiting Puerto Rico. Her and a friend."

"They were my first patients my first night as a doctor in Puerto Rico," he said and drove on. "The first people I lost."

TWENTY-FOUR

AFTER A FEW MILES, they coasted into the town of Aguadilla, on the north westernmost corner of the island. She held onto his hand in silence after visiting Doña Sara. Julián's life seemed book-ended by grief. His devotion to the island exposed him to the worst in everyone. The loss of two young girls on his first shift was unimaginable, an experience that created bonds she'd never comprehend.

They agreed to a quick afternoon coffee, so they turned off the main road, straight north, past the western end of the old Air Force runway from almost ninety years ago.

The change was drastic. A mile from the old military road, signs for sub developments with catchy names sprung up, out of place and ubiquitous. Half a mile later, fields lay choked with weeds and garbage, followed by another massive subdivision with an even more banal name. The cycle repeated for miles, a patch-work of remote opulence squeezing out what was left of nature and the locals.

Julián drove up to a converted home that enjoyed its heyday a century ago. The porch, painted bright teal, lay under a sleek holo sign.

"I always thought they should call this Venn Cafe," he said under his breath as the car locked. "You'll see."

Coffee was the lifeblood of Puerto Ricans, at home or abroad. Surprising to most outsiders, the island tradition was deep and focused. Real coffee existed only in a handful of varieties: negro (black), *pocillo* (a long espresso shot), *ralo* (watered down), cortado (with a splash of steamed milk), or *con leche* (with milk). Some deviation was allowed, but the manufactured insanity of "venti triple skinny half-caf pumpkin spice with soy" just did not exist here.

At least, for anyone who was a local.

This cafe was an affront. The delectable aroma of Puerto Rican coffee mixed with the sweet tang of fresh bread made her mouth water and her stomach rumble. But the board atop the counter, garish and out of place, blared out impossible drinks no self-respecting Puerto Rican cafe would carry. Naturopathic crap and genetically modified infusions crowded the menu, overshadowing the standard local fare. This shop appeared to be the bastard child of a mom-and-pop shop and a trendy rip-off joint. The menu of imported faux beverages reminded her less of blending and more of disease.

They ordered, avoiding the jug-sized drinks with flavored milk, and sat at a little table on the porch. A fan blew misted, scented air, pushing away the heat.

"What do you think?" Julián asked as he sipped his cortado.

Isabel shrugged. "Didn't expect it to be this good from that blue hologram thing on top of the counter."

"Whenever I come here, I like to think that all that other crap will go away, but fifty years from now, I'll still be able to order a cortado."

She tried to smile. "If the coffee shop is still here."

"If Puerto Ricans are still here," he added.

They were silent for a minute. "What is with all those access control neighborhoods on the way here? Is there some big employer out here?"

He shook his head. "That's why I wanted to show you this. Aguadilla is the next Dorado. If it isn't already."

"What do you mean?"

"Most Puerto Ricans can't afford to live where they're born. Expats are scooping up a lot of property. To their credit, they fix things up, but when they rent it out, the locals can't afford it."

"Who does?"

"More expats. Who can buy everything because they don't pay taxes."

"Are they investors? Millionaires?"

He took a sip of coffee through a grimace. "These days, mostly trust-funders and nepo babies. They scoop up property here and claim to live on the island."

"Julián, please explain to me how the hell the government thinks this is a good idea. To have super rich people move here, buy everything from under the locals, then expect us to pay the taxes for them. This is insane."

He flashed a curious smile. Instead of responding, he turned to a couple returning to their EV. Their dress, jewelry, and disdain marked them as expats.

"Hey, excuse me," Julián said in unaccented English. "Are you guys in the act sixty crowd in Aguadilla? I'm coming from Raleigh and need to connect."

The girl—oxy skinny, with fake boobs and blond hair streaked purple—rolled her eyes at them, annoyed at the interruption of her weekend coffee excursion. The guy sounded like he was still stoned from the previous night.

"Ask your AI for 'agua dealers.' You know, like dealing water."

Julián nodded thanks, and the guy entered his EV with a wave. He must've been doing well because in Tampa, that EV went for two years' worth of MBA salary. In Puerto Rico, it would've cost twice as much.

The couple screeched out of the gravel parking lot and sped north. Isabel's stomach knotted in anger.

"He could run someone over, stoned or drunk, and nothing would happen to him. Am I right?"

He nodded. "I see the results every week."

"Why? Back stateside, that asshole would've been a joke. A fucking stoner living in a basement trying to get rich off some bullshit crypto scheme." She sat up and drilled into his eyes. "Here he's a wealthy prince with some strung-out slut by his side. What are we bringing on ourselves?" The duality of Puerto Rico simmered everywhere she looked. The entire scheme—come to the island to avoid paying taxes and contribute nothing in return—felt so wrong that she ground her molars until they hurt.

Julián shook his head. "Here." He brought his watch close to hers to share the link. She blinked twice to accept.

Some asshole had posted a selfie video blasting down the highway on his EV, panning over as his date wiped white powder off her nose.

"Get off the road, you fucking beaner!" The camera shuddered as he blasted past someone on a loaded bike. The man's face, a mix of shock and amusement, reappeared on image.

"You almost killed him, asshole," the girl said.

There was more. The site, catering to expats coming to the island, was the most condescending compilation of media she'd ever seen. The page was blunt about everything she feared: how much to bribe to escape local drug charges, where to find prostitution disguised as partner swaps, updates on skirting residency requirements through blockchain, and the easiest places to score coke, tranq, and oxy. But what boiled her blood, what hurt most, was their vision of the locals. Videos of blighted buildings, the narrator berating the lazy ineptitude of those born here. Unfettered whining about substandard conveniences and third world infrastructure they had wrought on the land. Clips of barely clad twenty-somethings partying on boats or penthouses, dripping with smug exclusivity and oblivious to the hellscape beyond their bubbles.

In minutes, one site—one of thousands—portrayed local Puerto Ricans as chattel: too stupid to be rich, pathetically incapable of success. The invaders believed their fairy tale lives were a birthright, and the indentured servitude of the locals an obligation. The Puerto Rico tax haven—created by the island's politicians—was fate's way of ensuring the scales tipped in favor of the gilded. The island, they believed, was ripe for their taking. Those born here were a minor inconvenience.

"I want to leave." Her murmur rasped with anger.

Julián nodded. Before standing, he leaned in close for a whisper.

"Remember Judío? Elodio?"

She clenched her jaw and nodded.

He pointed his thumb behind him, in the direction the scumbag couple had left. "Those bastards sold our island to them."

The anger started deep, spreading through her like ink in a storm. Instead of despair giving way to tears, something different erupted inside, something that made her shake.

Fury.

"Now you know," he whispered.

He reached out for her hand, and they walked away from the teal porch, away from those who thought themselves gods, from those who did not know that millennia ago, the island had its own.

TWENTY-FIVE

THEY TOOK the long way back to San Juan, heading south past Mayaguez on the western coast. They took a detour to Rincón, the westernmost tip of the island, on a single road cutting through a jungle. Isabel had never seen this part of Puerto Rico, home to the best beaches and resorts. After meandering through the town of Aguada, they slowed to a crawl. Ahead, a steel arch proclaimed the entry into Rincón.

She teased Julián with a gentle push. "Guess a bunch of people had the same idea?"

He didn't smile. After a few moments, they reached the arch and realized it was an entry control point. Two armed guards, dressed in tactical gray for the heat, approached the car on either side, motioning for them to lower their windows. The cool fragrance of tropical blossoms wafted in the breeze.

"Hi. We're just visiting," Isabel said. The guard on her side said nothing, waving his watch over hers.

The two men exchanged something before the other guard stepped back and raised his rifle.

"She can come in. Your passport is no good."

She couldn't inhale. "What do you mean? We're only passing by!"

"This is private property, ma'am. Locals can enter only on official business."

"We only want to see the town."

"The zone of Rincón is private property."

She wanted to spit and yell and insult the men, but this was not their fault. They, too, would not be granted passage into the largest tourist preserve in Puerto Rico. She tapped her phone to stop the document broadcast and glanced at Julián.

"I just wanted you to know." He turned the car around and drove past the parade of foreigners queuing in line to enter a part of his home.

Julián Almodovar—a physician educated abroad and serving his birthplace—was a second-class citizen on the island of his birth.

A few miles south, everything burst. She wept, empty and lost, gazing at the Atlantic Ocean as it bled into the Caribbean Sea. The emerald hills and luscious beauty of her birthplace were fleeing from her grasp.

Their grasp. The curse for those doomed to be born in paradise was having their home flayed from them, a torture decades in the making.

She wiped her tears and felt his hand on her forearm.

"I'm so sorry, Julián. I'm embarrassed. This is not what I expected. This is so unfair—"

"No. I'm sorry." He squeezed harder. "I'm supposed to show you the island.. Instead, I dumped every injustice on you, showed the ugliness everyone hides."

She placed her hand on his. "I'm glad you did."

"It was inappropriate." He pulled his hand away and shook his head, his eyes far down the road. "You're going through a lot. You don't need me to dump all my anger on you."

"Julián, please."

"I hate this. I hate what has happened to us. I hate bottling it up. Before you, no one cared. No one questions. They're just—"

He slammed his hands on the steering wheel, causing the instrument panel to beep a short warning. A thin tear streaked down his cheek.

"You okay?"

He wiped the emotion before she could reach it, which broke her heart. "It's okay. I'm sorry."

"It's alright. Tell me."

They sat in silence for miles. She draped her wrist on the center armrest. After a few minutes, he clasped his hand in hers. He didn't say a word as he drove, half on autopilot, until they turned into the mountains north of Ponce.

"I'm trying, Isabel. I swear to God I'm trying."

"I know," she whispered and covered his hand in hers.

The past day had heightened her to every dissonance. Darkness crept from the mountains, but too many cars drove with missing headlights or weak orange embers struggling in the dark. Halfway into the twenty-first century, these cars still parted the night with incandescent bulbs. The bluish LEDs of more advanced vehicles— powered by electric motors, like every damn car back in Florida— were notable for their rarity. Why not?

Those who owned everything had already retired to their bubbles to bask in excess. Those who catered to them were only now going to—or returning from—work. Her island had become a playground for the global rich, and those born here had somehow become their servants.

"Do you work tomorrow?"

He shook his head. "First day off in three weeks."

"A Monday off. Could be worse."

She played with his beaded bracelet, gazing out into the constellation of patchwork lights peeking from the mountains. As they swooped into Caguas, both the traffic and roads worsened.

The sense of decay and poverty transformed into a new awareness. This wasn't the result of chance or misfortune. It was purposeful neglect, the result of an incompetent and corrupt government scamming the citizenry for years, selling their blood and soul to retain power.

This time she did not miss the sign stating Entering Private Property when they entered Condado from the south. This puzzle was now clear. No local policemen roamed these streets, no shootings or drug abuse occurred in broad daylight. A few blocks away, the situation was a combat zone. The horrors of daily life in Puerto Rico were meant to be contained far away from the gilded.

"When did they sell Condado?" she asked, no longer surprised.

"Only a few years ago. The Act 60 guys bought most of everything here and in the end, told the government they'd do security as well." He pointed in the dark to a dark shop between a nail salon and a CBD dispensary. "That's the last local business left."

"That's why everyone's a tourist."

"The expats don't want us to mingle with them. Like in Rincon."

The shame in his eyes crushed her. Doctor Julián Almodovar had everything: he was intelligent, kind, selfless, and devoted to something much greater than him.

And he was a second-class citizen in the place of his birth.

He pulled up to the hotel lobby to drop her off. The armed security guards—she now knew them to be private police—nodded as the car stopped.

"Thanks for today," she whispered. "I cannot thank you enough."

"You saw how things are. No filter."

"Would you walk me in? I just don't feel right with..." she tilted her head at the men.

He parked and accompanied her to the elevator. They rode up

in silent understanding. Julián stopped at her door and held her hands.

"Thank you."

"I should be saying that, Julián, not you. I had a wonderful day."

He stared at the carpet. "Thank you for listening. I didn't know how badly I needed to say all of that."

She squeezed his hands.

"It's not all bad. There's always hope. I don't want you to leave with this image in your mind. You've been through a lot and don't need me dumping my frustration on you."

"I feel like I've known you my entire life," she said with a smile. "And I cannot thank you enough for sharing everything with me."

"I could talk to you for hours."

He leaned in for a goodbye kiss, caressed her cheek, and turned to go.

She pulled him back and kissed him, deep and hard. Then she opened the door, shut the world behind them, and fell into his arms, desperate to make him remember.

TWENTY-SIX

SHE WOKE to the buzzing of her watch.

Julián was gone.

She sat up, holding the bedsheets over her breasts. A sharp chill cut through the confusion. They'd fallen asleep together, and she woke up alone. Her dress was still under the small table, where she remembered tossing it. Her bra dangled from the chair that started the most unforgettable night of her life.

But his clothes were missing.

Her watch buzzed again. She cleared a strand of hair from her face and sighed with relief.

JULIÁN ALMODOVAR

I'm outside with coffee. Can you let me into the elevator?

She tapped her watch to buzz him in and looked around her room. Her ears burned remembering last night.

He'd be here in minutes. She leapt out of bed, hoping to find something to wear. She was brushing her teeth and washing sleep off her eyes when she heard a knock on the door. Her heart stopped.

She wrapped a towel around her, ran a hand through her hair, and said a silent prayer, hoping he would not run away.

Please, God. Please don't let him regret this.

She opened the door, covering herself with one hand. He stood unmoving, holding a tray with coffee and a box from the cafe next door.

"Well, good morning. Are you trying to tell me something?"

"I look terrible."

"Wow." He blew his cheeks out. "That was not the word I'd use."

She tried not to burst into laughter and pulled him into the room.

The towel dropped when he kissed her. She fell onto the bed, naked and open.

"Please kiss me," she breathed.

"I just want to remember you like this."

She did not let him go. Her body smoldered long after they caught their breath.

"I think the coffee's cold," he said, caressing her back.

"We have a microwave," she murmured into his neck.

"I thought I was being all gentlemanly by surprising you with breakfast."

She giggled in his ear. "I liked breakfast in bed."

The guava pastries made a mess on the sheets, and the coffee tasted better after they reheated it. She kept pulling the sheets up to cover herself, but Julián kept pulling them down to stare. They laughed and teased each other as the sun climbed into the sky. After a while, she excused herself to clean up for the day. He joined her in the shower until the chime interrupted them.

Isabel, still wet, pulled on a dress to confront the cleaning crew.

The lady regarded Isabel's damp hair and clinging fabric and left with a knowing wink.

She shut the door behind her, stifling a giggle. Julián peeked out from the bathroom.

"Oops."

"Don't apologize. We spent so much time in bed that now I'm hungry."

"My treat," he replied. "Where should we go?"

She gazed at the shimmering heat rising over Santurce and beyond. "I want to see the politicians outside their cages."

The change in his voice was immediate. "Why?"

She pulled him close and held his hands. "You've been an angel. You've shown me the good and the bad of a place that lived only in memory. I've seen how my people—your people—live as second-class citizens in the land of their birth. I want to meet the people who did this." She pulled him in tighter and clenched her emotions back. "I want to know who of us did this."

"We've spent a beautiful morning together. Why now?"

"Because I want to see it with my own eyes."

She rubbed his back as they stared out the window, south into the world.

"Okay. I ask only one thing."

"Anything."

"You are beautiful." He caressed her cheek. "And strong. And anywhere else, you'd be a queen or CEO or diplomat."

Then he squeezed her shoulders, and every spark of joy left him.

"The people who destroyed our home don't care. Please be careful what you say. I can't believe I'd ever tell you something like that, but please try to understand."

She pulled him in tight, burying her face in his chest.

"I want this to be the start of many beautiful days, Julián. I'd never risk that."

TWENTY-SEVEN

HEAT SPILLED from the concrete canyons of Santurce, blasting them in a blinding, late-lunch glare. Julián parked the car at a lot a block away, where a tired man with few teeth and skin made of wood exchanged a small card for cash. Isabel had seen more dollar bills in the past three days than in the last five years. In Puerto Rico, cash was still king: untraceable and untaxable, thus indispensable for the small percentage of the locals that still worked for a living.

The smell of waste and urine shocked her, so close to what passed for a decent restaurant. The construction surrounding them narrated the takeover of San Juan. Blocks of gleaming structures loomed over lots covered in weeds, waste, and cracked concrete. Among them stood concrete structures from early in the last century, their joyful paint faded and chipped in the relentless sun. The island's past seemed old and faded, replaced by a shiny, contemporary and alien future, one where she did not belong.

The restaurant reminded Isabel of island reels from the 1980s. Carved wood and cheap plastic adorned the entrance. Beyond, an unremarkable square expanse of low gray ceilings and walls adorned with anonymous Spanish art. It must've been the place where grandparents came to relive the good old days of drinking during work, escaping family life, or meeting a mistress.

But Julián had insisted it was the perfect place: inexpensive enough for the local politicians to come in, with just enough selection to make it worthwhile to the expats who'd stick their nose at anything the local might afford.

The proprietor, a corpulent man ten years older than them, nodded a hello at Julián as they walked in. Her cheeks flushed when the man shook her hand and declared, in a thick Castilian accent, that Isabel was "preciosa."

"*Aquí, por favor.*" They sat next to each other at a small square table near the back of the restaurant. The room had no tables close to the windows where passers-by could peek in. This was where people came to hide.

It took her almost a minute to realize the menu was the paper card on her table. She leaned into Julián for a whisper.

"Do we have to pay in cash here, too?"

"I think I can pay with my watch," he replied with a wink.

They nibbled on pan sobao dipped in a magnificent olive oil and took in the scene.

"That's the deputy head of the development bank. What's left of it."

"I thought that went bankrupt when I was born."

He shook his head. "They buy bad debt, repackage it, and sell it around the world."

"Who the hell would buy that? Puerto Rico hasn't had a balanced budget in forty years! The oversight board will be here for forty more!"

He looked around them and leaned in. "People in the hedge fund world. People who know that bankruptcy is the most lucrative business in Puerto Rico. Especially when AIs pump out a believable and fictitious prospectus."

"Who is he?" She pointed with a stealthy pinky at a short,

greasy man—an expat—sitting with an elegant local woman with exquisite makeup and ridiculous boobs. She was doing her best to use the buttons on her blouse as a weapon.

Julián rubbed his nose with his fist to cover his mouth. "Two-time expat. Brought some money from Sarasota, big investigation. Cooled off for about ten years, and now he's back."

"I'm sure he's paying no taxes."

"You would be right. Recognize her?"

Isabel shook her head, and Julián pinched his nose before answering.

"She's the secretary of justice in Puerto Rico."

She stared back, slack jawed. "This is disgusting. I could take a photo and shut her down."

"No you couldn't." He flipped his phone over and swiped to open the camera.

"More secret soldier stuff?"

He nodded. The camera image was a jumble of static. She tapped her glasses to capture the snap, only to see a SENSOR OFFLINE warning blinking in her periphery.

"Never thought I'd see that," she murmured. She'd heard of "buzzers," devices to safeguard secrets and slow down digital voyeurs. Some kid at MIT had discovered that at the right modulation, the imaging processor on phones and glasses took on too much noise and shut down, rendering any image capture a messy blob. The young entrepreneur left school during his junior year and made a billion selling the technology to someone Isabel forgot. All she remembered was that the technology was exclusive, rare, and expensive.

And this restaurant had it.

As if on cue, the owner appeared at their table with a friendly bow. "May I take your orders?"

Julián asked about the specials, and the owner smiled when

Isabel announced she had no food allergies. "I would recommend the risotto with pig's feet."

"Are you serious?"

"Absolutely. It is criminally good," he said with a wink. She smiled at the choice of words.

Halfway through the glass of wine, the waiter brought out their plates. She'd never ordered anything like this and hoped her adventurous spirit did not result in a gastric disaster.

It took one bite. The dish was the most sublime meal she'd experienced during her life on planet Earth. Each bite was a blanket of savory perfection, and she had to focus on relishing every mouthful lest she eat the massive serving in two gulps.

"How are your meals?" The owner asked between trips to tables.

"Dios mío," she replied. "I thought you were exaggerating. This is the best thing I've ever had in my life."

The man smiled with pride. "I'm glad you like it. We've been making it since you were born."

Cold washed over her. "How'd you know when I was born?"

Julián placed a warm hand on her forearm. "Look around you."

She glanced around the restaurant, at all the middle-aged lechers hitting on married women, the old guys who thought they owned the world, the despicable hags that sneered at her in disdain.

The owner leaned in and whispered. "Nuestra Isla se está muriendo. The young stand out for their absence."

A breath caught in her throat. *Of course.* Twenty-five years ago, Puerto Rico had over three million residents. In an ever more crowded world, the island had lost half a million residents—almost one-sixth of the population—in only a decade. Those who could flee did so at the earliest opportunity. In their place, rich expats from the mainland took their spots but contributed nothing to society. The few who remained tried to move forward in an environment where public investment in their futures was the lowest priority, where remaining in power was job one.

Her island was dying. She glanced into the owner's eyes and understood. He knew it too. The shame of having to pander to those raping his birthplace cracked his tired eyes.

She wanted to say, "I'm so sorry," when she noticed two burly men with bulges under their coats enter the restaurant, straight to their table. She held her breath when they gazed around, waved a finger over their heads, and a slight man appeared behind them.

He was too well dressed, too emphatic, too sleazy, and he called out to them by name.

"Doctor Almodovar and Señorita Isabel." Hearing Elodio Santos utter her name shook her core. "What a surprise to meet you here."

TWENTY-EIGHT

"MISTER SANTOS," Julián nodded. "You remember my friend."

Elodio curled his lips into a chilling smile. "I do. The independent investor."

Her heart stopped. "Yes. My family."

Elodio gazed at each of them. He glanced at the proprietor, who left them without another word.

"When were you born, Señorita Isabel?"

She took a sip of water before answering. "A few days before Hurricane Maria."

"Yes. Of course. Then you might be too young to remember."

Julián squeezed her knee under the table and smiled to hide the terror.

"I have had an interest in this island's... economic development. For quite some time."

I bet you have, she wanted to answer, but nodded instead.

"Some would say I was witness to the beginnings of this current golden age of the island's growth."

She wanted to ask what golden age, but remembered Julián's admonition. "I can imagine," she said instead.

"Everything we see out there—all the construction, all the new homes, all because of foreign investment in the island."

"There's a lot of high-end construction," she answered, and Julián squeezed again.

"Yes, indeed. Requires a lot of capital. And many investors."

"That's why I was —"

"Of which you, and your family, are not."

Her breath caught in her throat, and the room swayed.

"Due diligence these days is so much more complicated. What with the bots flooding the web with nonsense, the yearly crypto scandals, and losers inflating their net worth. Dios mio. But in some cases, it is far easier. An investor who does not understand how this island works, who to reach out for help... well, perhaps they're not a real investor."

She took a sip of water to stop shaking.

"Someone who does not understand how to get things done— who bypasses and ignores those who only want to do the best for them? Perhaps they might not be entirely honest. Don't you think, Señorita Perez?" He bowed and touched a hand to his heart.

She froze, unable to even blink.

"And our automated assistants are so helpful these days. Why, it took no time to discover that you, Isabel Perez, are the daughter of a cop who abandoned us after Hurricane Maria. Not someone worth my time."

Julián squeezed again, but she shoved him away. "My dad did *not* abandon the island. The island abandoned him."

"Niña, por favor. We needed security, and your father tucked tail and—"

"My father was paid twenty dollars an hour to sacrifice his life for a government that knew poor cops were easy to buy." She stood up and leaned into him. "He moved us to Tampa so his family could survive."

Elodio Santos leaned into her. "You are still poor. And by definition, an idiot. Not an investor worth my time. You committed the gravest sin: you lied to me."

"You've lied your entire life."

His smile was the vilest thing she'd seen. "And who would care? Who will you tell? Who would believe you instead of me?"

She was about to tell him when Julián stood up to separate them. "Mister Santos, our apologies. We should go."

"No, we should not," Isabel replied. "He walks in like he owns this place and starts badmouthing my father." She glared at Elodio. "I don't care who you are. You have no idea what we've been through, or how many have left because of people like you."

"Perhaps I don't." He curled one side of his mouth in disdain. "Possibly because I don't care. My apologies. I should not have intruded. Please," he gestured at the table. "Enjoy your lunch."

He bowed his head and walked off. The two men with him— thick, with bulks under sport coats unnecessary in the tropical heat —fell into step ahead of him. A few steps away, Elodio turned.

"Oh, and by the way. Send my regards to your Titi Luisa. Hope she gets better soon."

TWENTY-NINE

"Fede! Can you hear me?"

Isabel glanced outside between sobs, watching the gray city fly past. She wanted to scream, to apologize, to die and leave, all at once.

The call finally connected—the mobile network was always overtaxed—and Fede's voice crackled through.

"I got the note. Bad news."

"I'm so sorry, Federico!" Isabel struggled to speak before breaking down again. "I couldn't sit there and—"

"It's okay. No te preocupes. This was bound to happen."

Julián reached out for her hand. His eyes were a storm—anger, frustration, and powerlessness. In one heated exchange, she had destroyed everything he'd built. Elodio Santos had not become the most powerful man on the island by building anyone up, or connecting, or excelling. He'd been the power behind four governors in Fortaleza because he knew everything and everyone—and because he was willing to destroy anything, anyone, on a whim.

Especially those who did not consider him irreplaceable.

"We'll have Titi out as soon as you arrive. Roberto will be here in five. The crew is ready to move out."

Isabel stiffened in the passenger seat. "Move out?"

"Not our first time," Julián replied. The transition from Puerto Nuevo to Guaynabo passed in a blur. They zipped through the checkpoint into Bayamón, another minor inconvenience on an island filled with them. Julián gunned the EV to the limit, the autopilot correcting just enough to avoid cars parked along narrow streets. Roberto's vehicle waited for them at the clinic.

She'd only been here at night and now understood how the hospital disappeared in plain sight. This part of Bayamón appeared blighted, with old, graffiti-covered concrete buildings still sporting rusting iron grates. The odor of rotting fruit hung in the air, but the closeness of the buildings provided some respite from the sun, even in the brutal humidity. A century ago, when these neighborhoods had been built, shade had allowed comfort in the tropics. Now, with yearly climate catastrophes, living inside a concrete apartment with no cooling would be suicidal.

Thus this empty quarter: the locals could not afford to live in the world their forefathers had created. The billionaires living in this tropical tax haven had no such problems: they could afford to burn the planet to keep themselves cool. That tragedy had a silver lining for Julián and Fede, allowing them to open a clandestine telemedicine surgery clinic for next to nothing.

Roberto shook hands with Julián and hugged Isabel. "Guess she's leaving?"

"Yes," Julián replied. "Both of them are."

Fede wheeled Luisa into the afternoon sun. Isabel tried to shade her eyes from the glare, wondering what people would think seeing an elderly woman on a gurney emerge from a rusted metal door plastered with graffiti. Her fears were unfounded: no one was around in the heat of this day.

"Isabel," Luisa whispered. "¿Como estás, bella?"

She squeezed her hand, kissed her forehead, and cried. "How do you feel?"

"Como coco. Cansada, but I'll get better soon. When we get home, I'll make you some *asopao*."

Before anyone replied, Federico cut in.

"Doña Luisa, we have some people waiting for you in Tampa. We must hurry to make the flight, so we're taking you directly to the airport. We'll have some people take care of your house."

Isabel's stomach lurched. Her inability to keep her rage at bay now had a face. Luisa, frail and weak, would have to leave the island. For how long, God only knew.

She reached out for Julián. "Are you sure we have to do this?"

He stopped to face her as the two men loaded Luisa's gurney onto the truck. Isabel expected him to be angry at her outburst. His eyes were raw from emotion—none of it directed at her.

"Elodio has probably been following you ever since the party. It was a big tell when you didn't jump at his offer to help. Took him no time to figure out you were lying." He glanced behind him before continuing. "He found out about Luisa. Which means he's been checking into you."

"There are laws for that, Julián. Digital privacy laws that—"

He stepped close to whisper in her ear. "Do you think people like Elodio Santos care about the law?"

"But how can he do that? No one has that capability?"

"Not an obstacle, if you know who to bribe."

She shut her eyes tight, holding the emotion at bay. "Why would he do this?"

He looked around before answering. "Because he thinks this island belongs to him. Those desperate to stay in power will destroy anything they can't control." He placed his palm on the concrete wall of his life's work one last time. "Elodio never heard about this clinic. He was unaware of what we'd built. Imagine if people could succeed without needing him to grease the skids in government. That would be his greatest threat."

"But all you're doing is taking care of people! On an island where everything left to the locals is broken and picked apart!"

"They don't care. All they know is we didn't play the game. We didn't pay him to be the gatekeeper. We were not beholden to them. That is a danger to those in power."

She doubled over, holding back the nausea. "What now?"

He shrugged. "Go back to Tampa. Take care of Luisa."

"What about you?"

"We'll rebuild. I'll try again. We've done it before, and we'll do it again."

She reached out for his hand, hoping he would not push her away. "I am so sorry, Julián. I can't believe what I've done."

His touch felt cold and distant, far removed from the memory of the previous night. "It's okay. It wasn't the restaurant. Everything started when Elodio asked about your past. I had no idea a white lie would change so much."

"I'm sorry—"

"It's not your fault, Isabel." He pulled her in. "Our island is the only place where dreams are crushed when others cannot control them."

THIRTY

"Do you have everything?" Julián asked.

Isabel nodded and squeezed him tighter.

He wiped a tear from her cheek. "You shouldn't waste pearls this way."

She draped her arms around him and tried to remember the scent of his skin. "I didn't know you were a poet, Doctor."

He smiled and caressed her hair. "I'll see you soon."

She stifled a sob on his shoulder, breathing deep to remember him. "I'll miss you."

"Go. Please take care of her."

She hugged and kissed him one last time, then turned to board the airplane. Fede waved as she followed the attendants who wheeled Titi Luisa into the boarding ramp.

This was not how she'd expected to return. Luisa, thin and frail after only a few days, remained attached to this land. Would she survive in Tampa? Of course, she'd have all the medical care she'd ever need. But what about her friends, her life?

That was the tragedy of those born on the island: leave for a better life and evade the horrors they lived in, or stay because they'd been born into something too precious to lose. Everyone honest with themselves knew the problems. Those who stayed did so because friendship, love, and family made life in hell livable.

She was torn between a deep hatred toward those who'd sold their birthplace for the illusion of power and love for so many who found meaning and fulfillment in the simplicity and gratitude of life. How could these two coexist? How could joy survive? Was that why so many had left? To bring that warmth and happiness with them, no matter how far they might stray from the island of their birth?

The attendants helped Luisa into her seat. The tickets back to Tampa cost a fortune, but Fede had somehow finagled a medical attendant fare. Most of the SSTs did not have beds in first class, since trips were so short. But subsonic transports still had them. Luisa had enough space to lean back, the IV pack snug on her upper arm.

She leaned to see the terminal as the lumbering jet taxied onto the runway, hoping to glimpse Julián one last time. She recorded a quick message before the pilots reminded everyone to stash their devices for takeoff.

"Thank you, Julián. You are unforgettable." She blew the most suggestive kiss she could muster while sitting next to her aunt, then stared out the window. The topaz ocean, endless and wild, made everything else insignificant.

The distance to Tampa was short enough that the difference between SST and subsonic was only forty minutes. But flying subsonic meant she'd be connected on the way back. She called her friend as soon as they leveled off. Luisa slept as brilliant white clouds glided beneath them.

"Paloma? Can you hear me?"

"Hey, chica. How's your aunt? I heard the insurance went through."

She related the entire trip, leaving out some of the more intimate details about her night with Julián. "What do you think?" Isabel changed the feed to her glasses and glanced over at Luisa.

"Oh my god! She looks so frail!"

"In just a few days, Paloma. I can't believe it."

"You want me to meet you in Tampa?"

"My mom is going to meet us there. I'd love to see you after we get her into Moffit."

Paloma's face filled the screen. "What are you going to do?"

"I'm not sure... We live in the most connected world ever, but all people hear about Puerto Rico are the beaches and the resorts. That's not how people live. Those who remain are living in hell. I saw dead bodies on the street. The few schools left open look like combat zones. The air is thick with waste and smoke. Insane luxury pushes the locals into poverty. The worst part? The tax cheats think they somehow deserve it. And the government does nothing."

"It's been that way for a hundred years, Isa."

"I know. But it cannot continue. Not after what I saw."

"So, what now?"

"I want the world to know."

Two hours later, they touched down in Tampa. The glint of solar panels on every home seemed surreal after so many blue tarps, tattered and bleached by the Caribbean sun. She received a ping on her glasses as the aircraft taxied to the gate: stay behind so EMTs could transfer Luisa without incident. By the time the engines spooled down, her aunt's medical records had been transferred, her vitals uploaded from the cuff on her arm. There was much to be said for modern medical science.

She met her mother Claudia at the gate, and they cried in each other's arms for a long time. Luisa held her sister's hand for the first time since they'd parted during a visit to Florida almost ten years ago.

Ten years. She'd been seventeen, convinced of her powers and her destiny to change the world. She remembered the first time Luisa held her hands after making alcapurrias for the entire neighborhood, when she confessed that in the Puerto Rico of 2036 power outages were still common, the government had yet to spend FEMA money, and the political class lost track of the annual crises of corruption. The Oversight Board would leave "soon," but the government had not produced a balanced budget in fifteen years.

Isabel remembered her outrage at the imposition. *I will change this*, she'd thought in the heated passion of a teenager. *I will return.*

She did return, and all she accomplished was to destroy the dreams of a brilliant young doctor with boundless passion and a soul that took her breath away.

The ambulance ride to Moffit was quiet and fast. The same doctor on the holo met them at the lobby and whisked her into a waiting elevator. Luisa blew them both a kiss, tickled at the attention. When the door closed, Claudia turned to her daughter, embraced her, and cried.

She rubbed her mother's back. "It's okay, Mami. She's safe now."

Her mother pulled back. "You saved her, Isabel. You saved your aunt. My sister. The last of my family. I am so proud of you. I thought I'd never see her again..." The words sank in a soft sob, and Isabel hugged her again.

After some time, Claudia wiped her eyes and smiled. "What did you think of our *Isla Bendita*?"

"*Isla Maldita* is more like it," she said with a sad smile. "I guess I had to see it myself."

"We've known for a long time. Every generation has to rediscover the truth. We're all born without memory, without sabiduría. I wish there were more like you."

"Me?"

Claudia shrugged. "*Juventud, divino Tesoro*. I wish the young would know what to fight for. Who to fight."

"What do you mean?"

"You saw it. For one hundred years, we've fought for a ghost. A religion that doesn't exist." She rolled her eyes. "We were worried about being the fifty-first state, or being independent, or inventing some new form of shared government. All that time we forgot that our political class couldn't administer a lemonade stand, that they wanted positions for power and money, not to help their country."

"Mami!" Isabel giggled in delight. "You sound like me!"

She reached out and held her daughter's hand. "When I was your age, I also wanted to save the world. Starting with my island."

She held onto her mother for a long time. "I want to tell the world."

"We live in a sea of information, Isabel. Finding the truth is harder now than it has ever been. In the middle of the twenty-first century, you had to go see your birthplace with your own eyes. We can no longer trust what we see through the eyes of others."

"I saw horrible things, Mami. I can't stay quiet. And besides . . . " She looked down. "When did you know?"

"Know . . . what?" Claudia stood back, regarding her daughter with a curious look.

"About Papi. When did you know?"

Claudia stroked her daughter's hair, tucking a lock behind her ear. "He was playing basketball with his uncle. First time I saw him, he was sweaty and disgusting. I knew immediately. There would never be anyone else." She caressed Isabel's cheek. "Tell me."

She took a deep breath and held her mother's hands. "I'm trying to be logical about this. I went through a lot with Titi Luisa, and my emotions are a mess."

"That's when you discover what you most need to know."

Her smile started deep in her soul. "I met someone who is

everything I hope everyone could be. Noble, and good, and devoted to something far greater than his fate."

"Is he handsome?" Claudia asked with a wink.

"I could stare at him for the rest of my days."

"I'm going to have to meet this young man."

"Someday, Mami, I hope you do."

THIRTY-ONE

"HOW'S MY HAIR?"

"Ay, nena, you look great," Paloma replied, eyes glued to her tablet. "Stop worrying about it."

"I want to look good. You never know when—"

"Por Dios, Isabel!" Paloma spread her arms in frustration. "You talk to him every day! And he was here last week! It's not like he's going to run away because your hair wasn't perfect on episode..." She swiped her tablet. "Episode 23."

Isabel rolled her eyes. "I'm just nervous. Today is six months."

"Ay bendito. Time flies. And how is Doctor Almodovar?"

"I mean six months for our show. Not for me and—"

"I know," Paloma said, raising her eyebrows. "I wasn't asking about the show. How is he?"

She tried to hide a smile. "He's perfect."

"You want me to leave for a minute so you guys can have some quick phone sex before we start?"

"Paloma!" Isabel felt her cheeks flush. "*¡Coño, no seas tan burda!*"

"I love you too, nena." She blew Isabel a kiss. "Ready?"

Isabel glared back and flashed her the middle finger. "Ready."

"Three, two, one." She gave Isabel a thumbs up and started recording.

"Hello, and welcome to Isla Maldita, episode twenty-three, the show about the truth behind the news in our beautiful home of Puerto Rico. I'm your host, Isabel Perez. Today, like every week, we'll talk about the latest developments on the island, and how you, in the Puerto Rican diaspora, can help retake La Isla del Encanto.

"First, some great news! We added two hundred thousand subscribers since the last episode, which is far beyond our wildest dreams. Since we have so many new members, I wanted to take a few moments to remind our new listeners and viewers about what we stand for.

"This is not a political show. We are not here to debate status, or political crises, or the latest entertainment news. We are held together by a common belief: that people born in Puerto Rico should not be fated to live a life of servitude, working for a growing population of billionaires who's only common thread is the desire to escape US federal taxes. We believe that Puerto Ricans deserve a functioning government, where politicians make decisions based on what is best for our island, instead of what is best for their pockets. And we believe that those who sold our futures to the expats and the hedge funds and the criminals should face justice.

"What Puerto Ricans—myself included—want to do with our future is our choice. But that decision can only be taken once our house is in order. We need a functioning government. We need to have fiscal responsibility and retake our fate from a well-intentioned but ill-fated oversight board. And we insist that the people who benefit most from Puerto Rico's intellectual capital contribute their fair share to the island's future. That doesn't mean building more homes for dilettante billionaires. It means investing in the land you now call home.

"If you are still with me after that, then welcome to the show. If not, click away now, because our next guest will blow your mind."

The episode finished, and Isabel cracked her neck. "How was that?"

Paloma swiped her tablet and smiled. "Dios mío. Nena, you were born for this. We had over ten thousand new IP addresses in the first twenty minutes."

"That's amazing."

"You hit a nerve." She tapped on her screen. "The aggregator counts over two thousand comments. Over ninety percent positive feedback, and that was just the first half of the show. Predicted subs for next week are up by seven percent."

"Wow."

"Wow? Seven percent growth in a week? That's faster than anything I've seen!" Paloma flashed Isabel a wicked smile. "You should celebrate with your beau when he flies up."

Her ears blazed. "Maybe."

"You're killing it, Isabel. You're making a difference."

They hugged, and Isabel peeled back the drapes to let the sun in.

The Tampa Riverwalk beckoned below. Sunlight glinted off innumerable solar panels dotting every visible rooftop, and EV's whizzed past, shuttling people from the airport, the bullet train, or Ybor City. Her adopted town, after years suffering under ideological idiocy, was now the Venice of the United States. She hoped that somehow, Puerto Rico could also escape the shackles of political ideology and embark on a path where democracy worked by expecting transparency and service from elected officials.

She felt the buzz on her wrist first and blinked to open the automated news feed she'd set up from San Juan.

BREAKING NEWS

SAN JUAN—A mass shooting has rocked the town center of Guaynabo, a suburban municipality southwest of the capital.

Initial eyewitness reports indicate a group of masked assailants, armed with automatic weapons, attacked a suspected riñonero clinic in an abandoned section of the city, a few blocks from the municipal center. Eyewitnesses accounts describe bullet-riddled victims dressed in white lab coats lying around what appeared to be medical equipment. A spokesperson in Fortaleza stated the equipment proved the occupants were performing organ harvesting, which is rampant on the island. The spokesperson indicated that the Puerto Rico Government takes citizen safety very seriously and has even outlawed telemedicine providers despite outcries from the AMA, MSF, and the ICRC. When asked, the spokesperson insisted the assault was not carried out by law enforcement, and that it appeared to be a turf battle between riñonero cartels.

Other sources dispute this claim, saying that the site was a clinic that provided telemedicine-based medical care to residents unable to receive help elsewhere. The source insisted that the "snuff job" was sanctioned by Fortaleza to eliminate competition with overburdened local hospitals. A Fortaleza spokesperson called the accusation "preposterous" and "unbelievable," insisting the report must've been manufactured by the opposition party to damage the governor's reputation.

In other news...

In an instant, she knew. Julián Almodovar, her soulmate, the man who made the world a better place and her life complete, was gone.

She crumpled onto a small patch of sunshine pouring through the window, sobbing under a slice of brilliant sky.

PART TWO
A DIFFERENT TOMORROW

PUERTO RICO, SEVENTEEN YEARS AFTER THE SCANDAL

2028: Ten years after Hurricane Maria, mismanagement of disaster recovery funds becomes front-page news in the mainland US. The GAO publishes a report claiming that 87 cents out of every recovery dollar have been awarded to firms related to a single island lobbyist. After a pre-dawn arrest, the lobbyist elects to cooperate with the FBI.

2029: Coordinated raids result in the arrests of thirty seven members of the Puerto Rico Legislature, seven U.S. Representatives, and three former governors. Diaspora protests erupt across major U.S. cities over the corruption scandal and related special treatment for Act 60 billionaires.

2030: Seventy percent of Puerto Rican officials resign under pressure from relentless federal investigations. The Governor steps down as investigations into decades-long mismanagement of Federal Funds dominate local news. The acting Governor then shutters half of the island's empty schools, reallocating the funds into tax enforcement and security. Half of the government's buildings, all empty, are sold or demolished.

2032: The acting Governor issues an Executive Order mandating review of every Act 60 decree. Six weeks later, she asks the Department of Justice for emergency support to investigate widespread Act 60 violations. Student to teacher ratios trend down as funds from closing schools flow into teacher salaries. Bunker fuel imports are outlawed in the aftermath of another Act 60 investigation. In exchange for lighter sentences, dozens of former political officials cooperate with the FBI and DoJ. Cooperation from jailed officials results in massive cartel arrests and an eight-year low in homicide rates.

2033: Fearing arrest for tax avoidance, 64% of the Act 60 population leaves the island. The FBI arrests seventy-two crypto "billionaires" for tax evasion and racketeering, seizing assets worth $32 billion. Authorities confiscate thirty-eight mansions, eleven business jets, seven yachts, and one private submarine to pay outstanding tax penalties. The recovered funds bolster security and tax collection, driving an unprecedented wave of diaspora returnees.

2036: The broadcast trial of three former governors results in massive protests, which drive new ethics and transparency legislation. New requirements for remaining Act 60 investors a wave of tech investment, dropping the unemployment rate to 2.7%.

2039: Based on improved tax collection and shrinking graft, the GAO predicts Puerto Rico will pay off legacy debt in fourteen to seventeen years. Local income tax is abolished for those below the top 20% of earners, replaced by luxury, real estate, and reduced consumption taxes. KO-KEE becomes the first generation of post-GPT LLMs created on quantum-enabled GPUs powered by renewable energy. Puerto Rico's population grows for the first time in a decade.

2040: Importing gasoline-powered vehicles is banned. New rules for carbon-neutral construction drives capital back to urban areas. The unprecedented urban recapitalization drops the unemployment rate in the Greater San Juan metroplex to zero. Massive tax breaks incentivize landfill reclamation, where companies race to extract rare earth elements, core metals, and other recyclables to meet high global demand.

2041: The *Tren Urbano* is converted into an expansive linear park called *La Sombra*. Small business growth explodes in the miles-long shopping, office, and lifestyle sector in the shadow of the former elevated train. Sales tax from *La Sombra* and luxury real estate tax drives the first fiscal surplus in one hundred years. Thoroughfares are modified with dedicated lanes for autonomous "street trains" with centrally-controlled traffic management.

2043: The last gas station closes in Naguabo. Puerto Rico builds the first piezoelectric taxiway at San Juan International Airport, then unveils autonomous vehicles for intra-city transportation. Student-teacher ratio drops below twenty. Labor participation rate grows to 58%.

2045: The Legislature passes its fourth balanced budget. Economists predict the Financial Oversight and Management will wrap up its work by 2047, thirty years after Hurricane Maria. Puerto Rico is projected to pay off its debt by 2055.

ONE

THE ENGINES THROTTLED BACK, slowing the craft below transonic as the aircraft descended into San Juan. Isabel Perez gazed at the brilliant ocean and emerald hills and caught her breath. She imagined a different scene twenty-seven years ago, days after her birth, hours before Hurricane Maria devastated Puerto Rico, when her parents took her from a birthplace she never expected to return.

Until today.

The jet descended low enough for her to recognize the outskirts of San Juan, simmering in glorious disorder. Gray sprawl emerged from the vibrant green of lush forest, covered with solar panels glinting on every available surface. Closer still, traffic moved on ribbons of black. Railings separated public transit lanes from the rest of the vehicles, zipping with the smooth trajectory of autonomy. The pavement under them gleamed with a dull metallic sheen.

She remembered a class in system design back in Gainesville, where Puerto Rico was lauded for taking a practical approach to public transportation: instead of building more roads, the government made it easier for automated EVs to circulate around the city.

Routes changed based on demand, controlled by an automated control center in Santurce.

She smiled with pride. Twenty-seven years after Hurricane Maria, after a painful reckoning with the past, her beautiful island was moving forward. Puerto Rico was now a beacon to the world.

The jet used every inch of tarmac to slow to taxi speed. It felt too big for the airport, even with wings swept back after clearing the runway. The taxiways were a deep black, and she could feel the difference in the pavement through the giant aircraft's landing gear. A dynamic display, shrouded from the bright sun by solar panels, announced something that made her heart soar.

¡Bienvenidos a Puerto Rico!
Welcome to Puerto Rico!
Today's arrivals have generated 217 kWh of renewable energy for La Isla del Encanto.
Enjoy your stay!

Piezoelectric plates—covered in recycled car tires rescued from century-old landfills—had replaced the cracked pavement she'd seen in old holos. The amount of energy generated was only enough to power a modest home for less than a week, but that wasn't the point. The message was clear:

We broke the code for living in the future. Welcome to paradise.

She disembarked into the humidity and blossomed into a sweat despite the frigid metal of the aircraft, still cool after the descent. The smells hit her first: the pungent scent of tropical flora, the comfort of coffee and pastries, the wisp of flowers, and behind it all, the sea. Then the sounds: aircraft engines spooling down, a cacophony of doves, the faintest hint of what she hoped was surf. Bright clouds fractured a deep blue sky, taming the brutal assault of the sun.

She stepped into a familiar world in the terminal. Everything moved, everyone yelled, people touched and laughed and hugged with a contagious energy. The lounge seemed a copy of the Puerto Rican cafetines sprouting all over Tampa, testaments to the diaspora that had sprouted in the years after Hurricane Maria. Scents of coffee and bread and tobacco and sweat and life covered her like rain.

She stopped at a deli for a quesito, a rolled pastry made with sweet cheese and sugar glaze, her favorite delicacy. She flashed her chip at the cashier, left a tip equal to the VAT amount, and walked out of the small shopping area before the exit to baggage claim.

The belts delivered suitcases of all sizes. She remembered something her mother had once said: you can recognize a Puerto Rican family returning to the island because they pack everything. The burly security guard helping a family ferrying massive suitcases probably thought the same. Her phone beeped, notifying her of her bag's arrival.

She popped the wheels out and strode out to the TRANSPORTE TERRESTRE area outside. The humidity slammed into her, bathing her in the odor of decaying seaweed and vegetation. People surrounded her, entering and leaving cars, embracing and kissing relatives. Public displays of affection were the norm on her island. Despite the oppressive humidity, she relished returning to what had once been her home.

An overlay proclaiming SCHEDULES came into view, and she tapped her glasses.

"Calle Sebastian Olano, Cupey."

The itinerary scrolled on her AR display. The next transport to Cupey would leave in four minutes. She blinked to find the location. Glowing arrows on her glasses pointed to a traffic island a few feet away.

As she crossed the street, she bumped into a woman.

"Ay, bendito, disculpe."

The woman smiled. "No te preocupes, nena."

"Can I help with your bag?"

"Gracias."

Isabel was about to lug the woman's bag onboard the street train when a young man intervened.

"Señorita, let me help."

He had the hard part and sculpted eyebrows typical of young Puerto Rican men back in Ybor City. She imagined the story, similar to hers: the kid's family moving to the mainland in the aftermath of Hurricane Maria, returning only after the cancer that had wracked the island had been purged.

She sat across from the woman. "Are you coming or going?"

"Coming back," the woman answered. "I went to visit my children in Atlanta. How about you?"

"I'm here to visit my aunt. I was born here, but my family left after Hurricane Maria."

"A lot has changed in that time."

"I know. My mom always told me how bad things were after the hurricane."

The woman nodded. "Those were hard years. But the past was held to account, Gracias a Dios. Look at us now."

She gestured outside. The driverless bus whizzed past the gleaming high-rises of Isla Verde and the glass towers of Condado, enroute to the freeway exchange headed south and west. The metropolitan area had been transformed. Gone were the garish billboards, the decrepit buildings, the crumbling infrastructure she'd seen in so many holos of the disaster.

In their place stood shiny new buildings of all shapes, terraced with plants and solar panels. Isabel could see the new-style windows—translucent solar panels—covering every surface. In terms of renewable energy, infrastructure revitalization, and urban reclamation, San Juan rivaled any city on the planet. Maybe, one day, she'd move back.

"So, I guess it worked," she whispered, mostly to herself.

"So far it has. It was either 'contribute your fair share or face the tax man.' You can imagine what they did!" The woman chuckled when her watch buzzed. "Well, here I go."

A soft ping announced the arrival at Minillas. The woman stood up as the vehicle slowed down, surprising Isabel with a soft squeeze on her shoulder.

"I'm glad you're back, *mija*. We need to rebuild. The island needs young people like you to return."

She stared back, unsure how to respond, when the woman made a sign of the cross. "*Que Dios te bendiga.*"

Seconds later the bus continued south, past Rio Piedras and toward Cupey. She glimpsed *La Sombra*, the former elevated train now converted into a massive linear park. A dozen sites suggested this strip had the best bars—and restaurants—on the island. Some huge AI company had cut the ribbon on a new lab under half a mile of park, marking the event with an obscene amount of *alcapurrias* for the invited guests. Some food critic from Miami wrote about the experience in almost religious tones. She spoke a note into her glasses to visit soon.

"I couldn't help overhearing." An older gentleman plopped on the seat across from her. "You haven't been back since Maria?"

Isabel shook her head. "I visited once, when I was five. Only for a weekend. Don't remember much. We've stayed in touch with my family."

The man nodded and raised his eyebrows. "That was right when everything started."

"Didn't that governor resign before that?"

"Oh yes. But the people who enabled him didn't go to prison until later. You were here as a child right when the arrests started."

The man smiled at Isabel's look and continued.

"That's when the Feds arrested that Elodio Santos guy. He began cooperating to save his skin. That was the first domino."

Isabel remembered the name, the most despised person in

Puerto Rico, the man behind so many scandals in Fortaleza. Puerto Rican neighborhoods in Tampa threw parties when he died in prison a few years past. "Wasn't that when the government collapsed?"

The man nodded. "Eight out of ten elected officials were either indicted or sent to jail. FEMA found out where all the money was going. And the IRS followed soon after."

"Why the IRS?"

"You may be too young to remember. There was a time when people would come to Puerto Rico, set up an address, and pay no Federal taxes. Except no one would check on them." The man laughed. "Can you imagine any government being that stupid?"

"I read it was pretty bad for a while. It's incredible to think people let that happen."

"The interim governor started to police tax cheats. She was smart enough to know that was the source of all the corruption. The big shopping malls hadn't paid real estate taxes for sixty years. Now, we'll pay off the debt in five."

"How much of the debt?"

"All of it. Once upon a time, mija," he said with a wink, "Puerto Rico was bankrupt. Hard to believe, huh?"

Shiny, compact EVs whizzed on the highway, while the bus— an autonomous overland train with an advanced control systems— zipped to their destination. The island was lush with new growth and construction sprouting from the endless green around them.

Everything was quiet, like in Tampa. Fossil fuel-powered vehicles were now illegal on the island. And everything was clean. She'd seen at least five scrubbers on the trip, cleaning plant debris, the result of frequent storms, from the roads.

"Who pays for all of this?"

"Amazing what happens when everyone contributes their fair share." The old man tapped something on his watch and shook his head. "Once upon a time, when I was not much older than you, only the middle class paid taxes. I still laugh at how stupid we all were to believe that could ever work. Now the rich pay their share." "What about all the construction?""These days, if you want to build a single-family mansion without solar, you can do it. But you end up buying three of these." He patted the seats and flashed a playful smirk.

The vehicle entered a shaded terminal and glided to a quiet stop. The gentleman helped Isabel with her bags. "Que Dios te bendiga," he said, then walked off to meet a delighted little boy who leapt into his arms. She followed the guidance on her glasses to a small bubble of a car. The outline of the vehicle glowed green as she scanned over it.

PEREZ, I. M. CALLE SEBASTIAN OLANO.

She blinked twice to accept and hoisted her bags into the mini taxi for the automated drive to Titi Luisa's house.

Work remained to fully segregate automated car lanes. The mini taxi did a great job nevertheless, weaving in and out of the driver lanes with minimal fuss. She marveled at how quickly her island had changed. Vehicle traffic had become secondary to pedestrian and bike paths. Ample sidewalks covered in solar panels provided shade to walkers and riders, and the curious lack of parking spaces around businesses meant the suburbs were designed for public transport.

After a few miles, the taxi climbed up a hill toward Luisa's neighborhood. She passed a curious structure in the middle of the road, awaiting demolition, which reminded her of an anachronistic sentry point.

The taxi dropped her off at the end of the street, a few houses from Luisa's. Most of the homes had been built in the middle of the last century—squat and stout, designed to survive hurricanes, not economic collapse. Now every house was painted in wild, earthy colors, the driveways graced with solar panel roofs sporting the logos of the latest in-house battery technology. People had given up trying to keep lawns in the tropics, so every home erupted with local blooms. The air hummed with legions of fat bees.

Up ahead, a group of boys and girls had set up a makeshift baseball diamond in the middle of the street. One kid whacked a pitch high in the sky, landing on a neighbor's solar panel with a loud *pong*. Half of the assembled crowd ran off in a mad scramble to retrieve the ball after its errant bouncing. The rest crowded around the batter—a skinny girl with pigtails tapping her bat on the ground—and the pitcher, an animated boy with wild hair and a leather glove as old as the neighborhood.

Isabel smiled. She hoped the kids would grow up together and never forget this perfect day.

The familiar-looking house seemed plucked from memory. A tiny EV sat tethered under a small but elegant photovoltaic sunshade, framed by garden planters blossoming with life. Before she could touch the pad, the door opened. Titi Luisa, smaller and wider and more lovely than she could've imagined, spread her arms wide.

"¡Isabel, my sobrina adorada! ¡Bienvenida a la Isla del Encanto!"

Two

She bent into the tiny woman's soft embrace. Luisa sobbed with joy, her gnarled hands caressing Isabel's face.

"Dios mío, you are more beautiful than any picture. Entra. Estás flaca."

Luisa closed the door and led them into the breakfast nook by the kitchen. The scent of candles, sweet bread, and local spice soothed her. Soft drapes cast lazy shadows as they fluttered in the breeze. Isabel propped her bag against a wall and breathed in the luscious smell of a home-cooked meal.

"Que Dios te bendiga, mi bella. How was your trip?" Luisa stuck a wooden spoon into a pot and stirred. "Are you hungry?"

"I'm starving. What did you make?"

"Arroz con cebolla. Your favorite."

Isabel sat down to a heavy plate. Luisa piled the dish—rice sautéed with onion, bacon, and spices until salty and sweet—next to a stack of tostones. The golden fried plantains still steamed from the pan.

"You still like jugo de tamarindo? It was your favorite when you were a little girl. Your mother told me they have it in Florida."

Isabel's mouth watered. Food had been the love language of the island for all of her life. Her mother might have lost her touch cooking Puerto Rican delicacies after decades on the mainland. Titi Luisa, Gracias a Dios, had not. Isabel gorged herself on the food, burning her palate, washing it down with tamarind juice and garlicky mayo ketchup.

"So, what do you think of your birthplace?" Titi Luisa asked. "I know you've seen all the pictures, but it is different when you're here."

"Not what I expected. So much has changed."

"For better or worse?"

"Much better. I know things had been rough for years, and despite the feeds, I didn't know what to expect."

Luisa laughed. "Everyone wants to go to heaven, but no one wants to die. We needed to go through rough times to achieve this. I'm glad I saw it before I pass."

"Titi! Don't say that!"

"Ay nena, everyone's time will come. I'm blessed that I lived to see my island recover."

"I was talking to some people on the train, and reading about it on the trip here."

"Did you take a taxi?"

She nodded. "One of the self-driving ones from the station in Cupey."

"Ay Dios mío! Those little things? I don't like them at all. That's why I still drive."

Isabel almost choked on the tamarind juice. "They're safe, Titi! They're everywhere in Florida."

"I don't care if they're safe. They're so lonely! You're traveling in a bubble with no one to talk to."

"A safe bubble that makes no noise and doesn't pollute."

"My car is quiet and doesn't pollute either. If I'm going to sit alone, I'd rather take the train." She waved a dismissive hand, then slapped Isabel on the hip. "You need some tembleque. You are too skinny."

Isabel squeaked a grin. "Oh my god, you are so sweet! That is my favorite!"

"It's in the fridge. Let me go to the bathroom, and you can tell me all about all the boys who must be crazy about you."

She rolled her eyes as Luisa disappeared down the tiled hallway. The tembleque—translucent, sweet coconut pudding, sprinkled with cinnamon—lay cooling in a heavy glass dish that must've been decades old. Her aunt was the fortunate member of a unique generation of humans: those who'd seen their birthplace recover from the abyss.

She savored the delightful tembleque when she heard a crash.

"Titi? Estás bien?"

Silence.

She dashed to the hallway, cold with fear. The old wood veneer door to the bathroom lay ajar. Isabel pushed and found her Aunt Isabel—the strongest, kindest woman she'd ever met—lying on the floor, blood seeping from her nose.

THREE

"TITI! Titi Luisa! Can you hear me?"

Isabel shook Luisa's hands, sensing a faint pulse through the clammy skin.

She fought the shakes, tapped on her glasses, and stared at the EMERGENCY icon in the corner. A red bar lit up.

BLINK TWICE OR SWIPE FOR EMERGENCY.

She blinked a dozen times, swiping the swoosh on her watch for good measure. She needed a teledoc now.

"State the nature of your emergency."

"I need emergency medical assistance."

"This is the AI medical program. A human doctor will be online in sixty seconds. Please place the victim in your field of view."

She stared at Titi Luisa, breathing slowly to steady the image.

"Image acquired. Blink to acknowledge patient ID or swipe for options."

She glanced at Luisa's name and information, then blinked to accept.

"Confirmed. Tap patient's watch to connect."

She tapped her watch on Titi Luisa's and a green dot lit up her glasses.

"Connected. Stand by." Seconds later, the AI continued. "Patient is alive. Pulse is slow, erratic and shallow. Patient appears to have suffered a stroke. Emergency medical care has been notified and is en route.

"Please ensure the patient is breathing. Do not move the patient until emergency medical personnel arrive.

"Please secure any medications the patient may have in the vicinity.

"Please note any injuries the patient may have suffered. Repeat: do not move the patient.

"Do you acknowledge?"

"Yes! When will they arrive?"

"Stand by. Emergency medical personnel will arrive in approximately ninety-seven seconds."

She shut her eyes tight as the tears burst, squeezing Luisa's hands tight until the AI chirped.

"Do not move patient until emergency medical personnel arrive. Please acknowledge."

"Sorry," she replied to the bot, and tried to slow her breathing.

Seconds later, footsteps raced behind her. A tall man with intense eyes and a neat beard motioned at her to step back. He scanned her watch as his partner unfolded a small suitcase into a spindly gurney that cradled Luisa and elevated her from the floor.

"Will she be okay?"

The female EMT scrunched her nose. "Too early to tell, but I think so."

"The AI said she had a stroke?"

The EMT nodded. "I'm sorry, but this is not uncommon among women her age. We have a lot of practice with this."

"Will she recover?"

The male EMT motioned Isabel to follow them outside. A phalanx of kids, their parents standing behind them, watched as they walked outside. A few were crying.

"Is Doña Luisa sick?"

"She's fine," the male EMT replied. "Got an owie on her head, but she'll be back soon. *Sana, sana—*"

"*¡Culito de Rana!*" the kids sang out through sniffs.

"She'll be back soon. Take care of her stuff, okay?"

The boy with the hair and the girl with the pigtails held hands and nodded.

The back of the ambulance looked like a mobile operating room. Most of the gear had been replaced with a handful of sensors and displays. The female EMT strapped something on Luisa's arm—Isabel recognized it as one of the latest medical devices from the war in Azerbaijan—and connected to the mainframe.

"And... we're up. Blood pressure is low, but stable. Pulse is eighty-seven. Oxygenation at 95%." They connected with the doctor on call, a breathtakingly handsome man a few years older than Isabel.

"Hello. Doctor A. Vivian and Roberto here. Can you hear us?"

"I have you loud and clear. Looking at the report now."

"Patient is a sixty-four-year-old female, presents unconscious with bleeding nose. Possible ischemic stroke. No signs of a slip or fall, no pharmacological indications."

Doctor A, whoever he was, nodded as he read something off-camera. "Got it. Stroke unit is notified. I'll do the admitting, then pass them off to the specialist. They'll evaluate for surgery. Anyone with her?"

"I'm her niece," Isabel whispered.

"Got it. See you all soon."

They retraced their trip north, to a hospital near Condado where she remembered her mom had been born. The drive back, as the sun set, passed in an eye-blink. The ambulance, under autonomous control, must've transmitted the route to cars on the road. She could not see outside, but could follow the trip through her glasses. The traffic showed bright red—standstill—but the ambulance blasted through, driverless, parting the river of cars. Traffic management in San Juan worked at least as well as in Tampa.

"Thank you both so much." She'd managed to control her emotions now that it appeared Luisa was stable. "I just arrived, and this happened."

"Where are you from?" Roberto asked.

"Born here, but live in Tampa. Haven't been back since I was five."

"I have a sister about your age," he said with a chuckle. "She's a nurse up in Charlotte."

"I love that city. Did she go to school up there?"

"UNC Charlotte for nursing. She was an undergrad at UF in Gainesville."

"No way! What year?"

"Graduated... five years ago, I think? Must be, cause that's when I got out of the army. I'm a terrible brother." He furrowed his brow. "You look just like her."

"She must be awesome then," Isabel replied with a wet grin.

The van doors burst open as the ambulance rolled to the Emergency entrance. A phalanx of techs wheeled Luisa out on the cool transformer gurney, returning a few minutes later and handing the suitcase back to Vivian, the EMT. A young man with a tablet motioned to Isabel to follow him to the waiting area.

"Thank you both," Isabel said and offered a hand. Vivian waved the gesture off and hugged her instead.

"I'm sorry you have to go through this," she said. "This is going to sound terrible, but this is a great place to have a stroke. Best care in all the Caribbean."

Roberto opened his arms and squeezed her in a muscular embrace. "I'll tell my sister I met a fellow Gator. And don't worry." He gestured toward the hospital. "I'd trust Doctor Almodovar with my life. Your Titi is going to be fine."

She nodded to hold the emotion at bay and waved as they sped off into the afternoon.

An orderly set her up in a bright waiting room stocked with real books, puzzles, and games. Isabel could not focus. She wanted to trust Roberto and Vivian, but could not wait to hear the diagnosis straight from the physician.

"Miss Perez?"

The voice belonged to the doctor from the van. Her world swayed, as if she'd known him for years. His eyes—soft and kind—ripped into her soul, taking her breath away.

"I'm Julián Almodovar. The doctor who admitted your aunt."

"Will she be okay?"

"She's fine. She suffered an ischemic stroke. Lucky for her, you caught it early. She's stable, being prepped for an operation right now." He smiled, and she knew everything would somehow work out. "This is a common procedure. We have a lot of experts on staff, and the hospital is set up for this type of patient. I can't promise anything, but her prognosis should be positive."

"Are you sure?"

"This is going to sound terrible, but we've become quite competent at stroke care in San Juan. We'll keep her for observation for a few days. You're visiting from Florida?"

"I am."

"I'd plan on staying a few days. We'll keep her for seventy-two hours after her procedure, to make sure she's okay to go home."

Everything came out at once. She collapsed, sobbing onto the chair.

"Hey," Julián whispered. "You okay?"

She nodded. "I haven't seen her in years. She's the strongest woman I know, then this happens, and..."

She grimaced, trying to control her emotions, and felt a caress on her cheek.

"You shouldn't waste pearls this way."

She giggled as she wiped her eyes. "I didn't know you were a poet, Doctor Almodovar."

"I'm sorry, Miss Perez. That was very inappropriate of me. And please. My name is Julián."

She sniffed again. "Please don't apologize. I'm Isabel."

His eyes narrowed. "Of course. It had to be."

"What do you mean?"

"Please don't take this the wrong way." He stared with a curious smile. "You are in a tough emotional state, and I don't want you to think I'm taking advantage of the situation."

"Just tell me!" she said with a laugh.

He held her gaze for ages. "I know we've never met. But as soon as I saw you, I've had this strange feeling that I know you. Not from before, but... from somewhere else. I can't quite put words to it."

She squeezed his hand. "Will you think I'm crazy if I tell you something?"

"Can't be any weirder than what I said."

"As soon as I saw you, I felt the same."

"Maybe we were separated at birth."

"Maybe we were separated somewhere else."

They shared a perfect silence before he stood. "I have to do the handover with the night shift," he said in a soft voice. "They arrive in a few minutes. It was an honor to meet you Isabel. I..." He stopped, trying to hide something, but his eyes betrayed him. "I hope you enjoy your time in Puerto Rico. Please take care of yourself."

He lingered for several heartbeats, squeezed her hand, then walked away.

There was a lifetime ahead of her, and it began now.

"Julián?"

He turned, and at that moment, she knew.

"Wanna grab a bite when you're done?"

AFTERWORD

In 2019, after the disastrous resignation of then-Governor Ricardo Rosselló, I read the most apt description of Puerto Rico's situation:

> *The Government of Puerto Rico is like a family member who is an addict. Congress is like their extended family.*
>
> *The addict has abused their spouse and children, lost their job, and spent all their money. Instead of getting them help—enrolling them into treatment, cleaning them up, providing education and helping them make the right choices—their family refinanced their credit card with a wink a warning: try to do better.*

This image perfectly encapsulates the death spiral of the island's government institutions. Congress approved an Oversight Board that elected to forego the structural change that would benefit future generations of Puerto Ricans. Instead, it has taken a back seat to the constant political scandals wracking the island, contributing only suggestions and exercising the occasional fiscal veto. They approve unrealistic fiscal plans that will never succeed, abdicated their role in economic development, and burned millions making Top Four consultants and bankruptcy lawyers rich. The bulk of their legacy has been to cement bankruptcy litigation as the single most lucrative profession on the island. Meanwhile, a generation of opportunists has razed—and raped—the island according to their whims, invisible to the erstwhile overseers of governance. Puerto Rico remains the only bankrupt tax haven in the world, an oxymoron for future economic textbooks.

Understandably, some continue to protest the Board, insisting that political change can only come from within. Those voices would be wise to reflect on that old chestnut: "The definition of insanity is doing the same thing over and over, yet expecting different results." Puerto Rico's political system has reliably failed its citizens for over one hundred years. Absent external input, there is no reason to expect differently in the future. Congress raised hopes for that external correction, but fell far short. The hopes for a bright tomorrow for native Puerto Ricans vanish by the day, even as the riches of those who used the island to avoid the IRS grow by the minute.

The Puerto Rico of today is not far off from the dystopia in Part One of this novel: a place of two tiers of rights, where billionaires play on land appropriated from the poor while the middle class pays their bills. Any defense of the status quo (*"Act 60 beneficiaries pay their fair share in local taxes"*) is predictable, farcical, and naïve. The reality is simpler: the Puerto Rican middle class pays an enormous amount in taxes as a share of their total income, while Act 60 expats pay a minuscule amount on their income—and the fortunes they hide from the IRS.

This is not entirely the fault of the Act 60 crowd: any capitalist would do the same. The blame lays squarely with Fortaleza. Their claims that these investors somehow benefit the public are amusing and insulting—unless one assumes that the only good future for native-born Puerto Ricans is to serve the rich and build their playgrounds. The Government of Puerto Rico has used graft and the sweat of a vanishing middle to fund a crumbling welfare state where over half of the island's population is doomed to inhabit. Politicians, meanwhile, bask in transactional and ephemeral power supplied by investors who consider the island their property. If we want to find the best example of economic hell on planet Earth, it isn't in some third-world petrostate or banana republic. We have one in America's backyard, the former jewel of the Caribbean.

I'd love to thank the many people who quietly provided input for this work. Alas, I cannot. The art of political persecution, and the pastime of focusing on irrelevant crises at the expense of what is important, are both alive and well in the island of my birth. I cannot in good conscience put anyone at professional risk by acknowledging their contributions to this book. I can say this: every person who saw the first draft of *Isla Maldita* had the same comment: it is far worse. What you hold in your hands is as much their frustration as it is mine.

Finally, I'll answer the question everyone asks: why is this book not written in Spanish? The reason is simple. This story is not meant for the residents of Puerto Rico: they know and live this tale. This is meant for the wider world: the policy analysts in Washington who might consider staying somewhere other than the Vanderbilt in Condado; the investors who already factor in "cost of corruption" into their proformas; the second and third generation diaspora who cling to a past which will never return. It is for the Congressional staffer who wonders how much money lawyers and consultants launder from the island's bankruptcy, and for those in the diaspora who bristle with disdain as yet another wave of entitled virtue signaling ignores the excesses of the island's political elite.

If this book makes anyone uncomfortable at how Congress incentivized economic atrocities to be imposed on American citizens; or inspired to resist the depredation of the most beautiful island on Earth—then the journey will be worth it.

∿

Did you enjoy this book?
If you did, would you consider leaving a quick review?
Reviews are the best way ensure other readers find the books they love.
Thank you.
We'd love to hear from you. If you have any feedback on this novel, please write to us at contact@atabey.press.

About the Author

Sebastian Faust is the pseudonym of a son of the island. Like many of his fellow Puerto Ricans, he lived through an endless stream of corruption scandals, wondering when the island might recover from the cancer that eats it from within.

This is not his first book, and will not be his last. He can be reached at sebastian.faust@atabey.press.

www.ingramcontent.com/pod-product-compliance
Lightning Source LLC
Chambersburg PA
CBHW030830020726
47499CB00006B/2144